Peace and blessings to the Wilkersons.

Best,
Kurt W. Smith
"Kay"

Lotus

KAY W. SMITH

ISBN: 978-1-4834-3413-1 (sc)
ISBN: 978-1-4834-3412-4 (e)

Library of Congress Control Number: 2015910622

Lulu Publishing Services rev. date: 07/14/2015

To my favorite men:
Patrick, Roman and Nolan, for your love and patience

To the world's best parents:
Eliza and Karry, for your unwavering support

And to the people who keep me sane:
**Karlisa, Karry (Jr), Bernice and Joy, for your
unapologetically-biased encouragement
and confidence in me**

"If you feel lost, disappointed, hesitant, or weak, return to yourself, to who you are, here and now and when you get there, you will discover yourself, like a lotus flower in full bloom, even in a muddy pond, beautiful and strong."

Masaru Emoto, Secret Life of Water

PROLOGUE

By the time the sun began to creep through the silk curtains, I had already been awake for three hours. My mind was no longer racing and for the first time in a long time, my thoughts were oddly quiet. I was strangely numb. Knowing that I couldn't avoid getting up any longer, my palms clenched at the sheets beneath me one last time as I tried to push down the nausea that was slowly trying to creep back into my stomach.

Rolling over, I shielded my face from the sunlight that was now beginning to brighten the entire room. It wasn't until I heard the loud snores coming from under the sheets next to me that I even remembered that she was there. I snapped out of my haze and began to contemplate how many times I might have to lie and say that everything was okay before the day was over.

Worried that my eyes were bloodshot, I reached for the pocket mirror that I had left on the nightstand next to me.

After blindly feeling around unsuccessfully in the dark for a few minutes, I started to run through all the excuses I would give if any of the twenty people who would soon be in my hotel room inquired about my appearance.

I'm overwhelmed with happiness.

I'm hungover from last night.

I'm nervous because I've dreamt of this day my entire life.

Another bad excuse was forming in my mind when I heard her voice.

"It's not too late to hop a plane to Mexico," she whispered from under a pillow.

I kept my back to her as I ran my hands across my pillow one last time. In case she turned on the lights, I wanted to be sure that the wet puddle that had formed through the night was gone. I took a deep breath before turning in her direction, conscious enough to avoid eye contact with her as much as possible.

"You're an idiot, Lola," I said, forcing a laugh as I kicked her from across the bed.

She peeled her night mask off her face and looked at me with the same sly smirk that I had known all of my life. Regardless of how much my sister loved my fiancé, Nicholas, I knew that she was serious and would hop a plane to Mexico at that moment if I asked her to.

"I'm just saying," she mumbled as she sat up in the bed and began to wipe her eyes. "Today marks the official beginning of the end of the rest of your life."

"Don't start, Lola." I shot back, secretly feeling more affected than usual by her anti-marriage joking.

"You are married and you are happy. Do you think that you are the only one who can manage to pull that off?"

I immediately felt guilty for snapping at her. From the look of the freckles that bunched around her eyes, I could tell that her feelings were hurt. I opened my mouth to apologize, but the look on her face said, "Trust me. I am your older and wiser sister"...so instead of making a big deal out of it, I decided just to let her talk.

"Yes, I am happy and no, I don't think that I am the only happily married woman out there," she said, trying her best not to sound defensive.

"But I would be lying if I didn't say that sometimes I miss having the freedom of considering who I am outside of being a wife and a mother. The little voice that pushes you to "find yourself" almost has to die a tragic death when you get married. Now, all of your thoughts and considerations have to include someone who has their own likes and dislikes, experiences and dysfunctions. Trying to be happy and make someone else happy isn't easy."

My sister had a special talent for giving the best advice at the worst times. Unsure of whether this conversation was going to have an upside anytime soon, I began to search for the room service menu. I felt knots returning in my stomach as I began to pace the room, scanning the pamphlet incessantly without reading it.

She didn't care that I was pretending not to listen - probably because she knew that I honestly was.

"That's why it's important to know who you are and what you want before you get married. If you don't, you will build the rest of your life solely around what someone else wants or needs you to be," she concluded with a satisfied tone.

With my back still toward her, I felt tears developing in my eyes. Tired of feeling like I was lying to her, I decided to tell her everything just as the phone rang.

"Probably your wake up call," she said getting out the bed and walking towards me. Before I could respond, she picked up the phone and demanded me to lie back down.

"I'll take care of it," she said, motioning towards the bed in her typical bossy demeanor. Now inches from me, I saw a flash of concern come across her face once she looked at my eyes. Before she could say anything, I quickly turned away and headed across the room to the bed as fast as I could.

As I walked away, I felt her gaze on my back even though I couldn't see her. Knowing that she was going to pressure me to talk once she was off the phone, I prepared myself to be completely honest with her. Seconds later she was fully distracted and in complete business mode - directing the front desk staff where to send the barrage of guests who would soon be on their way to my room.

Just listening to her direct the sequence of the morning's events, I couldn't help but admire the effortless confidence that she always conveyed. She never asked for anything; she only pleasantly demanded it. Since we were children, I secretly marveled at her ease in which she always seemed to get what she wanted, including the Ph.D. that she had by the time she was 26 and the perfect husband and child that she had by the time she was 30.

Once she was off the phone, neither of us said anything. I started flipping through the channels, hoping that she would not bring up our previous discussion.

Even in the silence, I could still tell that she was examining my face from afar. It was impossible for me to hide anything from her so I knew if she badgered me hard enough, I would say everything I didn't want to say. With less than four hours remaining until I walked down the aisle, I didn't want to take the risk.

"Lotus."

I immediately interrupted her, "Do you think we should order more fruit and pastries for the other bridesmaids?"

"Lotus," she repeated, now walking back towards me on the bed, "What's wrong?"

As soon as she wrapped her arms around me I started to cry. I felt guilty for worrying her, for acting like everything was okay and for being anything but happy on my wedding day.

As she wiped the tears from my eyes, I couldn't lie to her anymore.

"Was it hard to let go," I paused midsentence, embarrassed of how selfish my thoughts felt.

She laughed. "Was it hard to let go of being single?"

Surprised that she hadn't figured out what was truly bothering me, I nodded believing that was a sign to say nothing. If she knew what was on my mind, she would be more upset than understanding, more disappointed than anything else.

"You never know if you are truly ready for anything until you do it. For me, marriage was the most impulsive decision that I'd ever made. I didn't weigh the costs or the benefits. I just married that man who I love and who I know loves me. Regardless of whatever you are feeling, trust that nothing is more important that."

For the first time since the night before, I smiled thinking of Nick. The one thing that I knew for sure was that I loved him. He had been there for me through some of the worst times of my life, so I cherished our friendship most of all. I never had to guess his feelings about me, and that was one of the qualities I loved most about him.

"There's the smile that I was waiting for," she said.

"Lotus, trust me. It's okay to be nervous. Remember, I threw up three times the day I got married."

We both immediately burst into laughter.

"In a few hours I will walk down the aisle in a beautiful dress in a beautiful cathedral to a man who has loved me more than I have loved myself at times. Despite all of that – the only thing I keep thinking about is that I'm not sure if I've ever asked myself what I want, regarding anything. Today of all days, I should be sure of everything. I should be as sure about whether this decision will make me happy as I am the details of the reception menu but – I don't know. In some ways, I feel like I accidentally tripped into this day. It doesn't feel like I completely chose it, and it doesn't feel like I deserve it."

Before she could respond, we were both startled by the knocking on the hotel door.

"Go to the bathroom and splash some water on your face in case it's Mom or one of the bridesmaids," she said, pushing me back towards the bathroom.

Just as I closed the door behind me, I heard the voices of the rest of my wedding party filling the room.

Within the hour, the room was filled with champagne, fruit, and almost every girl who I loved most in the world. The conversation that I began with my sister felt like a distant memory. Mother entertained everyone with stories of her wedding jitters and Lola didn't miss the opportunity to mouth the words, *I told you so*, several times from across the room.

After my makeup and hair were complete, my wedding planner ushered me alone into the bathroom to put on my dress. Once I slipped into the silk organza gown, I considered the hundreds of times throughout my life I dreamt of this day. Looking at myself in the mirror, I pushed every remaining worry that I had out of my mind and focused on Nick, hoping that he would think that I was as beautiful as I felt.

When I stepped out of the bathroom in front of everyone, my mother and Lola were the first to cry. Tears began to stream down my face and for a few moments, and no one else in the room said a word. My mother hugged me tightly and whispered, "She is here," in my ear.   Seconds later, the wedding planner announced that it was time for everyone to go downstairs because the transportation to the church had arrived. Everyone filed out of the suite and soon Lola and I were left alone again. Waiting to receive the call from our parents regarding our separate town car, I opened the curtains and stared at the busyness of the city below.

Everything felt surreal. I was lost in my thoughts watching the flow of the taxicabs and moving cars below me when I felt Lola standing behind me.

"Lotus, what were you going to ask me earlier?" she asked.

I ignored her question.

"Before I interrupted you—after you started crying. You were about to ask me how did I do something, but I interrupted you."

I closed my eyes and pushed the thoughts of him as far away as possible.

"Lotus," she persisted. This time with more urgency in her voice.

With my back still to her, I wiped away the water that was collecting in my eyes.

"I honestly don't remember," I lied, relieved when someone started pounding on the door.

I walked past her as she stood in the middle of the room. When I opened it, my parents were waiting with the happiest smiles that I had seen on their faces in a long time.

"We tried calling, but your phone must be off the hook. The Lincoln is downstairs waiting for us."

Holding my hand out to her, I smiled at Lola, who was still standing in the middle of the suite.

"Looks like the getaway plane to Mexico will have to wait until after the wedding."

As the four of us rode to the cathedral, I saw that the day couldn't have been more beautiful. When we pulled into the driveway of the chapel in the center of the campus where Nick and I first met, every memory that led to this day slowly began to piece themselves together in my mind.

From a distance, I peeked through the open doorways, and I could see my bridesmaids lining up ahead of me. Hearing the pre-processional music begin, Lola didn't say anything; she just began to walk quickly in their direction. After a few steps, she ran back to where I stood waiting.

She cupped my face in hands, "Lotus, forget about the past and you can't worry about the future. All you have is today."

Looking her in the eyes, I could tell that she knew.

She didn't say anything, and neither did I. Like so many times before between us, words weren't necessary. We both noticed that the music had changed again, and she turned to walk away.

Once she was in front of the church she looked back at me, and I smiled. Even from a distance, the look of worry that she tried to hide spoke louder than anything that either of us could have said.

The 1ˢᵗ Trimester

ONE

Just think about Mexico, I kept telling myself as I tried to block out the loud voice and overpowering smell of stale breath in front of me.

It had been nearly six months since our honeymoon in Cabo San Lucas, but I tried to imagine myself back in the private ocean villa where Nick and I had spent two weeks. He had planned every detail of our trip meticulously, and it was endearing to see how much thought he had put into the entire ordeal. Every morning we discovered a new café for breakfast and every evening we fell asleep with sangria and cigars on our patio overlooking the ocean. My mind began to drift to our first night together, but I pushed the thought out of my mind. Thinking back, I had spent fifty percent of the trip with no clothes on, and being naked was exactly why I was in this situation.

"I don't need anything else. You are enough."

Nick whispered those words to me every night while we were there, but they had been cycling through my mind all morning. At the time, they were the sweetest things that I had ever heard, but now they felt like premonitions that taunted me.

As the yelling in front of me got louder, I felt my chest tighten. I was a pro at hiding my panic attacks, so I braced myself for what was going to happen next. I fixed my eyes on the pitcher of water on the table and began to sing the theme song of my favorite 1980s sitcom, The Golden Girls, in my head.

And if you threw a party –
Invited everyone you knew –
You would see the biggest gift would be from me…

Humming to myself, I tried to get my brain to convince my body that it was not about to die. Droplets of sweat started to form on my forehead just before my stomach began to churn.

The executive director yelled again and I could smell the smoked salmon bagel spread on his breath from across the table. "When I call, people answer. When I send for you, you come."

I scanned the room to make sure that no one else noticed that I was in a quiet panic. As he continued to yell, I strategized how I could get out of the room without embarrassing myself.

As I tried to ignore the feeling of imminent death, I couldn't decide which was worse: The sound of the phlegm that was stuck in his throat or the slew of spit that landed on the donuts in front of me every time he yelled. The only thing that kept me from completely freaking out was that I refused to give him the satisfaction of believing that the pressure of the job finally had gotten to me.

Between his arrogance and the patronizing tone with which he spoke to anyone with breasts and a vagina, he represented everything that was wrong with men in power. I had only worked as his managing director for a year, but people who observed us usually thought that we had been enemies all of our lives. We clashed on everything from professional ethics to sports teams to office decor. On most days, I suspected that others in the organization saw us as a train wreck waiting to happen.

I had heard people in our office speculate in hushed voices that we had dated in the past but that was the furthest thing from the truth. The real reason I disliked him was far simpler: He stole my ideas and presented them as his own every chance he got. He also secretly referred to me as "Sugar Tits," behind my back.

I dreaded every time he called me into his office to remind me that he was the newest face of the city's most prominent political party. I cringed when he would insist on riding with me between meetings so he could chain smoke and repeat things he heard on public radio. I even kept a small bottle of cognac in my desk, just to help me get through private meetings with him.

I despised him and everyone in the room knew it.

Think about Mexico. Just think about Mexico.

Closing my eyes, I took in a deep cleansing breath. Despite my feelings for him, I admitted that my angst was coming from another place. The events of that morning played through my head from the beginning, when my phone's calendar prompted me to pick up my next pack of birth control pills from the pharmacy.

For three extra train stops, I stared blankly at my cell phone. I recounted the days since my last menstrual cycle twenty times before convincing myself that my calendar had to be wrong. I had checked my work calendar, my pocket calendar, and the personal calendar on my tablet before I accepted that my period was officially a week late.

Pretending to listen to the discussion taking place around me, I went through every potential explanation in my head one more time.

It could be stress,
or premature menopause,
or cancer
or glucose intolerance.

"Shit," I said aloud.

The room grew silent, and every head turned in my direction. From across the table, the executive director's eyes bored into my forehead. I returned my gaze to the table, without acknowledging anyone, pretending to focus on the documents in front of me.

The sound of the mucus clearing in his throat made my skin crawl.

"Lotus, do you finally have something to add to this discussion?" he asked, sitting back in his chair with a patronizing smile.

Feeling all the eyes on me, I had to say something.

"*Sh-ouldn't* we consider the long term operating cost of the project before we try to convince our partners to invest?" I replied, secretly hoping that my words were remotely relevant to the discussion. Ignoring the gurgling in my stomach, I forced myself to smile and to appear poised, because confidence was the only language that the men in the room understood.

The look of annoyance that came over his face instantly made me feel calmer and more focused.

He stared at me for what seemed to be an eternity. A few of the gentlemen around the table chuckled under their breath. I wanted to look away, but if I did he would take it as a minor victory. It felt like this was the longest minute in my life until the silence between us became so deafening that the others in the room began to shift uncomfortably in their chairs.

Even with my heart pounding out of my chest, I refused to blink.

Finally, he backed away from the table and smiled. As if the exchange never happened, he turned his back to me and began to address the others in the room, exactly where he left off.

He reached into his suit jacket's inner pocket and pulled out a cigarette. Without lighting it, he placed it in the corner of his mouth and continued to speak.

"Listen. You know me. I know how to get the right people in the room to make something happen. If you can raise a million dollars for the Foundation, I can guarantee an up-and-running tech jobs program that will serve the entire city by the end of the year. I'll make sure that this serves each of your interests. And if we do this right, we can all get rich and help a few people at the same time."

He turned and looked directly at me. Though his smile brightened, I was sure that I saw two horns develop on top of his head.

"Trust me. You will want to be on the right side of this. You never know, you could be talking to the next political leader of this city."

The room erupted in applause, and I thought I was going to vomit. The sole woman on our board of directors was on vacation in Greece, making the testosterone in the room feel more overwhelming than usual.

I stood from my seat so abruptly that the chair fell backward to the ground. Pretending to gag, I bolted for the door, covering my mouth. Once in the hallway, I sprinted as fast as I could to the restroom, ignoring our elderly receptionist and other office staff who were in my way.

I locked the door as soon as I got in there and fell to the ground. Knowing that I would have to lie and say that I had a bad case of food poisoning, I emptied out the plastic basket that normally held extra rolls of tissue and placed it in my lap. I moaned loudly in case someone was at the door listening.

Every few minutes I made sound effects as if I was puking. Once I was sure that all the eavesdropping outside was likely over, I bit into a roll of tissue and yelled.

Is Nick ready to become a father? Am I ready to become a mother?

That was the thought that superseded everything else. Unlike Nick's position on parenthood, I always wanted to be a mother. Becoming a mom ranked as high on my bucket list as getting my JD, climbing the Himalayas and getting married, but I didn't want to fall into motherhood simply because it was supposed to come next on my life's to-do list.

I had only just begun to feel comfortable in the role of a wife; so the idea of taking care of another little human being was something my brain had difficulty wrapping itself around. I never doubted that I could become a great mother…eventually…but the mere mention of a baby conjured feelings of an impending apocalypse. Though I had the basics of what every woman thinks that she might need before becoming someone else's mom, a small part of me still felt like I hadn't fully began to live my own life yet.

With my head still submerged in the basket, I thought again about Nick's words to me while in Mexico.

I don't need anything else; you are enough.

Even when he said it, those words felt like an unspoken expectation to be perfect. Up until now, I had come pretty close. I had played the role of supporting wife – celebrating his accolades even as my career made me feel as if I was dying on the inside. He tried his best to be equally encouraging, but I had started to recognize the look of frustration in his eyes when I left a private law firm to work in the public sector and then again after I eventually left a respected post in the Governor's Office to work for the Foundation. He would never say it, but I often wondered whether he was disappointed in my failure to match his professional stature since the only thing more important to him than me was his career.

It has to be stress.

This single thought replaced all the others as I began to calculate all the reasons why my life wouldn't be able to accommodate a hypothetical child. Trying to recall if I had missed taking the pill in the last month, I could hear my gynecologist's ominous pre-nuptial warning in my ears: Get an IUD. Better safe than accidentally pregnant.

Feeling mentally drained, I lifted myself off the ground, thinking about the last night of our honeymoon. Though Nick and I had long ago agreed that we would have no more than two children, it was on that night that we decided to wait a few years before starting a family because of his plans to teach abroad. A small part of me resented that our decision was made primarily for his career goals, but I didn't argue. Starting fresh in Europe seemed like the perfect way to spend my last child-free years.

I splashed cold water around my eyes and prepared myself to face the stares from my coworkers once I opened the doors.

It has to be stress, I reassured myself one last time, confident that God had no interest in throwing my life into chaos. Considering that my chance of being pregnant was at least fifty percent, I decided to wait a few more days before mentioning anything to Nick.

What's meant to be will be, I whispered to myself as I glanced in the mirror one last time. Though I tried to ignore the sinking feeling that remained in my stomach, deep down I suspected that everything in my life was about to change.

TWO

6:00 a.m.

The alarm clock went off, and I rolled over to see Nick awake, staring at the ceiling. Most of Michael Jackson's "Beat It" blared through our condo before he lifted his arm to press snooze. As I watched him continue to stare blankly towards our coffered ceiling, I considered telling him that my period was now officially two weeks late. Before I could muster the courage to say something, the alarm's snooze time ended and another Michael Jackson song began to blare through our room. After a few more minutes, I waited for him to say something about my staring at him so early in the morning but he didn't. As usual, his mind was somewhere else, distant from our cozy, South Loop condo that overlooked the snow-covered Lake Michigan.

Like so many times before, I wished that I could read his mind. I ran through my best guesses of things that could be bothering him but came up with nothing. He had just submitted a proposal for a teaching fellowship in Paris, so for the past month we had innumerable talks about economic theory and planning potential road trips through Europe. Despite the stress of preparing his research for the review, most days he appeared as if he didn't have a care in the world.

With the arrival of our first holidays together as a married couple, things had been great as we playfully committed to using all of my bachelorette gifts before New Year's Eve. From the scented candles to the bedroom board games, we enjoyed our lives as honeymooners. I had enough La Perla to last a lifetime, but I jokingly dressed up in various costumes, just for kicks, which he seemed to enjoy.

He continued to stare off into an invisible abyss, and I knew it was pointless to ask him if everything was okay. In the five years that we had been together he rarely became upset or acknowledged even being agitated. As a self-proclaimed neurotic, I found his perpetual composure to be completely foreign. Though I admired it, at times I wondered whether he was utterly incapable of feeling intense emotions or whether he had just become very good at hiding them.

As I canvassed his body from the side, it occurred to me that my new husband was a far cry from the lanky doctoral student I had met in graduate school. His shoulders had grown broader. His body was toned from top to bottom. He had grown facial hair, which aged him but in a good way. He was smart, handsome, and confident, and always made an extra effort to make those around him comfortable. His humility was his most defining and attractive feature, but I had long ago noticed that he knew how to use it to influence people.

Finally noticing my stares, he turned towards me and gave me a kiss on the forehead. Looking into his dark brown eyes, I felt completely protected. Though I would never tell him, the truth was that I still couldn't believe that we'd ended up together. Most of the time, he felt like my fairy-tale and worst nightmare balled into one - a man so perfect that I worried relentlessly about how to keep him.

Looking back at the clock, he jumped out of the bed and stood gazing down at me. As I watched his eyes travel over my body, I decided that this was the moment of truth. It was his last day of classes before the university closed for winter break. He would have nothing to do but be with me through the rest of the holidays.

"Nick," I began until I saw him staring at my hair. I was instantly irritated because I could predict what was going to happen next.

"Lo, what's our plan for your hair? I thought you were thinking about growing it longer? This British-invasion mop top thing that you've got going on is cool, but maybe you should try something sexier in the new year?" he said, laughing to himself.

Before he could finish, I threw a pillow as hard as I could towards his head.

"Are you seriously criticizing my hair at six o'clock in the morning?"

He laughed, giving me his typical response. "If you wanted me to grow my hair out, I would."

"Okay, honey, what else would you like me to do? Should I get butt implants before noon?" I responded sarcastically, upset with myself for beginning to feel slightly self-conscious.

"Implants sound wonderful, just don't touch those boobs because they are perfect," he said with a grin before going into the bathroom.

Listening to him sing off-key in the shower, I remembered telling my mother that I knew he was the one because loving him "felt easy" although recently that didn't always seem to be the case. For better or worse, he was unapologetically honest, and that was the only thing he had ever asked of me in return. In exchange, he gave me what I needed – love, affection, and the assurance that he would always be there.

Now out of the shower, he dressed and sat on the bed next to me.

"I still love every piece of you, no matter what, Harry Potter haircut and all."

He leaned over and kissed me goodbye. Reluctantly returning his kiss, I decided to give it one more day before I told him anything. Minutes later, I heard our front door close and was grateful for the solitude.

The plush white down comforter on our bed tempted me to go back to sleep. Knowing that I would never make it to work on time if I did, I paced around our home, unable to fully relax. After a few failed attempts at meditating, I began to repeat the mantra that began the innumerable yoga classes that I had taken in my early twenties.

I am.

I am.

Before I could repeat it a third time, a quiet voice in my mind whispered back:

I am pregnant.

Giving up, I looked at the treadmill Nick had given me the Christmas before that had been collecting dust in the corner of the room. I had run the Chicago Marathon with my sisters the year that we met and for years I waited for him to ask me why I stopped running, but he never did. Instead, out of the blue, a treadmill appeared in my bedroom last Christmas with a bow on it.

I couldn't remember the last time I ran but for the first time I felt compelled to break-in the machine. Not knowing what type of shape I was in, I started the treadmill slowly, prepared to jog until it was time to take a shower for work.

Forty-five minutes later, I was running at full speed. Though my head was pounding, I remembered how much I always appreciated the stress relief of the sport. Hoping that I wouldn't regret it, I decided to push myself a little further.

Having hit a comfortable stride, I reached for the television remote to check the weather. Instead, what I saw made me come to an abrupt stop.

In front of me was my executive director, staring back at me through the large screen. Though it was snowing, he stood on an elevated stage in front of an abandoned school. He was speaking to a crowd of children, disabled veterans, and homeless people.

I turned up the volume just in time to hear him say, "In the footsteps of our sixteenth and forty-fourth presidents, I am proud to announce my candidacy to be the next senator from this great state."

After his announcement was complete, he began to chant, "It's our time" with the crowd that stood behind him.

Before I could process what I was seeing, the song, "Living in America" begin to play. When I saw him kneel down to pick up a baby from the audience, my body slowly began to sway.

Before I could grab on to anything, my legs buckled, and my feet slipped from underneath me. His face was the last thing I saw before a piercing pain shot through my body as my head hit the ground.

THREE

"Has anyone checked the carbon monoxide detector?" A familiar voice asked from above me.

I thought I was dreaming until I heard Nick's voice.

"I don't know if anyone has checked. Isn't that your job?" he responded in an irritated tone. "I've been trying to wake my wife up for the past five minutes, so can you please go and look?"

I sluggishly opened my eyes to see my husband, two paramedics, and our building manager standing around me. They were discussing how Nick found me on the floor of our condo. He explained that he had gone to the gym that morning and returned home only because he had left graded papers on the nightstand.

I eavesdropped from the floor as he recounted calling 911 after unsuccessfully trying to wake me. Our building manager, a skinny woman in her forties with garishly dyed red hair and the weathered look of an ex-smoker, emphasized that she came up with the paramedics only to make sure that everything was okay. Even with one eye opened, I could see Nick rolling his eyes. She was known for being nosy and a gossip, so the entire building would likely hear everything about my fainting episode by the end of the day.

They continued to discuss my condition as I lay on the floor with an oxygen mask covering my mouth. I tried to remember what had happened, but the only thing I could recall hearing was James Brown's voice before my head hit the floor.

I could see the television remote lying inches from my head. I could feel that I was wearing only one gym shoe. I could also hear the treadmill running behind me. Peering down, I was mortified to see that I was still wearing what I slept in, a sheer tank top and my favorite pair of My Little Pony underwear.

"I'm okay," I mumbled through the mask as I sluggishly tried to lift myself from off the ground. "I just overexerted myself."

One of the paramedics immediately began to kneel next to me.

"Ma'am, please lie back down."

Ignoring his plea, I steadied myself on my feet.

"Mrs. Price, you suffered a temporary loss in consciousness and we don't know how long you were out. You shouldn't be on your feet until you can be examined by a doctor at the hospital," the other paramedic asserted, now holding on to one of my arms.

I immediately resisted. "I'm pretty sure that I don't need to go to the hospital."

The building manager chimed in. "Honey, please do what they say. You may feel alright but if they think you should go to the hospital then you should go."

"Thank you all for your concern, but I'm fine. I'm not going to the hospital. No offense, but I truly hate them. If I don't feel well later, I promise I'll call my doctor," I said to Nick, hoping that he would agree with me.

"You need to go to the hospital," Nick interrupted while typing something on his phone. "Don't worry about the cost of the ambulance; that's why we pay for insurance. I'll ride to the hospital with you, but I might have to leave since we are in the middle of finals."

Accepting that no one was going to side with me, I wrapped myself in the blanket that had been on the bed.

"Do I have time to get dressed first? Or do I have to let the entire building see my 'My Little Pony' underwear?" I asked.

"We'll wait," both paramedics responded without cracking a smile.

I shuffled to the closet to grab a pair of jeans and a sweater before I slipped into the bathroom to get dressed. Once I was fully clothed, it hit me that within hours I would know whether I was pregnant or not. Relieved that Nick would be at the hospital with me, I was grateful that there would be no surprises, and there would be no need to find a way to tell him. We would find out together, for better or worse, and the relief or shock would be experienced equally by each of us.

I pulled my hair into a ponytail and walked back into our bedroom. He was on the phone, and once he saw me, he gave me a look that I had grown to know all too well.

I didn't try to hide my disappointment.

"Go to campus. I'm fine. I'll ride in the overpriced limo to the death chamber. I'll let you know the results if there is anything to tell."

It was obvious that he felt bad even though we had been through this many times before. He was on a tenure track, so he had taken on more classes and served as an advisor to a ridiculous amount of research projects. Though I had become accustomed to saying that I didn't mind his absence from things that should have been important to us both, it made me question once again whether he could ever be fully committed to anything other than his career.

Hugging me, he said, "Lotus, I'm sorry. Call me as soon as you see the doctor. I'll call your sister and ask her if she can meet you there, okay?"

We both walked out of the bedroom to see the building manager and the paramedics waiting for us in the living room.

"Sir, can you tell me which emergency room you plan to take her? Will she be at the university's hospital or Christ Presbyterian?"

"Neither," the more serious of the two responded. "Lakeshore Memorial is the closest hospital, so that's where we have to take her."

When I heard the words "Lakeshore Memorial Hospital" I thought that my heart was going to jump out of my chest. A wave of nausea washed over my entire body again as I tried to fathom whether the day could get any worse.

It must have shown on my face because Nick immediately noticed.

"Your hands are trembling," he said. "And your face is completely flushed. Do you feel lightheaded again?"

"No, I'm fine. I think I'm just dehydrated from running," I lied, knowing there was no way that I could tell him the whole story in front of these strangers.

Looking beyond the others in the room, I squinted my eyes to see Lakeshore Medical's sprawling medical campus through the windows that encircled our living room. I had spent so long pretending that it didn't exist that I forgot how close to it we lived.

Though there was no way for him to know why, I wanted to beg Nick to come with me, but there wasn't enough time to explain why Lakeshore Memorial Hospital was the last place he would want me to be, especially today of all days.

FOUR

DECEMBER 2004

"I won't let you fail. Just trust me."

When he said those words, it was the first time I realized that I might be in love with him.

My immediate discomfort must have been apparent. Nervously, I shifted my chair a few inches away from him and began to flip through the pages of my class notes. Before I had time to think of a response, Gabriel laid his hand on top of mine and said, "Don't worry. You will be fine. I promise."

Each time his knee brushed mine underneath the table a small flutter went through my stomach. I buried my head deeper into my textbook though I knew he was watching me from across the desk. It wasn't until we were midway through our study session that I finally glanced at him over my rimless frames and replied, "Thanks."

I was close to failing advanced calculus, which meant I was also at risk of losing my academic scholarship. Gabriel, the teacher's assistant, offered to help, saying that he couldn't live with himself if a girl from his hometown failed Dr. Foucher's class on his watch. We started meeting twice a week, but as finals approached, he recommended that we meet more often. Though I hated the idea of learning anything else about derivatives, I liked the idea of seeing him more.

In the weeks that we spent together, we had somehow become friends. I looked forward to laughing with him between my problem sets just as much as I prayed that I would learn enough not to fail the class. Regardless of how many times I offered, he refused to let me pay him for his help. The only payment he said he would accept were celebratory drinks the night that I passed the final exam.

A few days before our winter finals we sat by ourselves in a nearly deserted library. After five hours of going over open intervals, local maximums, and local minimums, I was exhausted. Deciding to call it a night, I turned to tell him that I was leaving, but saw that he had fallen asleep on a stack of books scattered in front of him.

Examining his face it was obvious why so many girls pined for his attention: He had the classic features of a model, the tall stature of an athlete and everyone knew that he was already accepted to Harvard Medical School. Though he carried himself more maturely than most other guys I had met in college, something about him also felt vulnerable and open. Just as my eyes glanced over his full lips, I shook off my wandering thoughts, mindful that we both needed to get some sleep for our early morning classes.

I nudged him awake. "Gabe, wake up. It's time to go. You can throw your bike in my truck. I'll drive you home."

Because of his popularity, most people thought he came from money, but I had learned the opposite was true. During our first tutoring session, he revealed that his parents were teachers at a high school close to where I grew up in Chicago. He also told me that, as the oldest of four children, he had worked since he was fourteen because he never felt comfortable asking his parents for money. Though he was in school on three different scholarships, he still struggled to accept his parents' offers to buy him a car. So he settled on staying in an apartment close to campus and depending on a Bianchi Vertigo bike that he named 'Lamborghini' to get him everywhere that he needed to go.

On the way to his house, I glanced over at him as his head rested on my passenger side window.

"Do you think your parents are still going to surprise you with a car for graduation? Before you say no, just remember that Boston gets pretty cold in the winter," I joked.

"If they do, they do. If they don't, they don't," he said, half asleep. "I managed this long without one, what's another four years in Boston with my sweet Lambo? She's dependable, she's cheap to upkeep, and chicks think she's impressive."

He continued with a smirk on his face, "Plus, she helps me to get rides from rich girls wherever I need to go."

I smiled back. "Well, in case you were wondering, I'm not impressed. I'll wait until after you graduate from medical school to see you in the real thing."

"I can impress you way before that," he said as he turned to look directly at me.

His comment was cloaked in innuendo, but I was caught so off guard that I didn't know what to say in response. Choosing instead to focus on the heavy snow beginning to fall on the road ahead of us, I forced myself not to read too much into his comment. After a few moments had passed without either of us saying anything, I turned on the radio to help pass the time until we got to his house.

When we finally pulled up to his apartment complex, I was relieved for him to get out of the car. I still didn't know what to make of his comment or the weird silence between us that followed, so I dismissed the exchange altogether.

Despite the blizzard, I got out of my truck to help him get his bike out of my trunk. After opening the hatch, Gabe looked at his watch and said, "Lotus, it's cold, it's late and it's snowing pretty bad. Your house is almost twenty miles away in the opposite direction. You need to stay here for the night."

My brain told me to bolt for my car and drive off as fast as possible. I appreciated the friendship that we had begun to develop, but it was hard to deny the feelings that I had for him. Dismissing any whimsical thought of us being something more, I looked at my watched and realized that he was right. I was exhausted and wouldn't make it home until well after 3:00 A.M. After a moment of hesitation, I agreed.

As I followed behind him up the stairs to his apartment, I reminded myself of all the reasons that nothing would ever happen between us. *He's graduating in less than six months. We are friends. He probably looks at me as one of his little sisters.*

I was still contemplating all the things that *wouldn't* happen between us as I watched him gather pillows and a blanket from his bedroom to sleep on the couch. Before turning to leave the room, he reached into his drawer and threw me his Harvard Medical School t-shirt.

"Here's to the future," he said. "It can get pretty hot in my bedroom, so this will probably be all that you need to sleep in."

Minutes later, standing in the doorway of his bedroom, I watched him make his temporary bed for the night. Afraid to step beyond the doorway because of how short the shirt was, I asked him if I could have a glass of water. After bringing me a glass from his kitchen, he refused to let it go. He stood so close that I could feel the warmth of his body though we somehow managed to not touch.

"Lotus, just so we are clear - it's important to me that you know without a shadow of a doubt that I want you. I've wanted you from the moment I first saw you. I don't want to be presumptuous and assume that you feel the same way, but I think, or maybe I just hope, that you do. If you don't, that's okay because I think I can change your mind. I'll be patient. I know that you will be worth every kiss, every stroke, every walk, every day – even if we just have the next six months."

He turned to walk back towards the sofa when I called after him.

"Wait."

As soon as I walked to him he pulled me into his arms. Nervous, I rested my face on his chest before I gently kissed him on the lips. Seconds later, I tried to pull back but he pulled me closer. No longer able to resist, we stood there in the darkness, kissing for what felt like an eternity. Before long, his t-shirt was on the floor, and my legs were around his waist as he carried me into his bedroom.

As we fell onto his mattress, he began to kiss me slowly from my forehead to my navel. His hands neared my waist and started to remove my underwear, and then suddenly he stopped.

"Lotus. I want you, but I don't want to rush."

Every inch of my body wanted to take things further. Looking into his eyes, I had no doubt that he wanted sex, but I could also see that he needed and wanted something more. Though we knew that we only had a few months, at that moment, it felt like we had forever to be together. Instead of making love, we fell asleep in each other's arms, surrendering to the feelings for each other that we had just confessed.

***

The following six months were a whirlwind. Soon it felt like everyone on campus knew that we were together – girls I previously assumed he was dating, guys I previously dated, even my calculus professor gave me an approving nod when he would see us together on campus. Outside of our classes, we spent every free moment that we had together - until the day that I watched him drive away with his parents to Boston. Despite the many conversations that we had before he left about scheduling Skype calls and visiting each other, I knew as he drove away that things would never be the same.

The following fall of my senior year, I was an exchange student at the London School of Economics. Between the five-hour time difference and our grueling school schedules, our nightly calls turned into weekly calls until we settled on sending each other an email every night. Naively, I thought we were doing great until I received a voicemail from him on Thanksgiving. I had decided to spend the holiday in Barcelona, so I was just returning home when I heard his message.

"Hey, Lo. It's me. I just needed to hear your voice," he began in a soft tone. "My mom is leaving my dad. Somehow they thought it was a good idea to announce it on Thanksgiving at the dinner table – right between the blessing and cutting the turkey. She just blurted it out. I don't know how to feel, but I just need to hear your voice. Call me back, babe. I love you."

My heart sank when I realized that he'd left that message six hours earlier. I called him repeatedly for an hour, but my calls went to his voicemail. When I finally got in contact with him that evening, his voice sounded emotionless.

"Come here after finals," I pleaded. "I'll get your ticket. I'll tell my parents that I'll be home after the first of the year since my lease isn't up for another few weeks. We can spend Christmas together, eat awful English food, get wasted and go to museums. Or we can just lie in our pajamas all day if that's what you want. Just please come."

"No. I can't," he replied flatly. "I need to come back home in a few weeks to help my sisters get through this. Look, I have to go. Have fun in London. My flight to Boston leaves tonight so I guess I'll see you sometime next year or whenever you get back."

Before I could respond, he hung up the phone.

In the weeks that followed, we never spoke for more than a few minutes at a time. He was always headed somewhere or needed to get off the phone to study. I was helpless, and I knew I was losing him. I did the only thing I felt I could do — I booked the first flight I could get to Boston.

I landed at Logan International Airport late on a Sunday evening and ran through the entire airport in a full sprint. For some reason I couldn't explain, as soon as my plane touched the tarmac, the urgency to get to him felt stronger than ever.

When I pulled up to his apartment building in Cambridge, I still didn't know what I would say once I finally laid eyes on him. I just needed to see him and to hold him. I didn't even wait for the driver to tell me the fare, I just handed him a fifty-dollar bill and jumped out of the car.

From a distance, a pizza delivery man was getting buzzed into the building, so I hurried behind him to catch the door before it shut. It wasn't until I started to follow him up the stairs that I realized that I hadn't eaten since I boarded the plane in London almost ten hours before. Famished and exhausted, I prayed that we were both going to the same unit.

As we climbed the stairs to the top floor, I heard the faint sound of soft music playing in Gabe's unit. For the first time since I watched him drive away from his apartment after he graduated, a sickening feeling filled my stomach. As the delivery man stood beside me, I raised my hand to knock on the door. From inside the apartment, I heard a girl's voice.

"I'm trying to surprise my friends inside. I'll stand over to the side until they answer," I whispered to the delivery man.

He nonchalantly agreed and pounded on the door twice.

As we stood there waiting for someone to answer, my heart began to race. I wracked my memory for the last conversation that I had with Gabe, trying to recall whether he had said he loved me or not, whether there were any indicators that he was ready to end our relationship. Just as I had convinced myself that the girl in the apartment had to be a friend, or a study partner, or perhaps a neighbor that he had befriended, the door opened.

"We've been in the bed for over two hours waiting for you to get here. We thought you lost our order," a girl playfully said before I heard her footsteps walk back into the apartment.

The delivery man looked at me with wide eyes as if he was prompting me to jump out and surprise her.

"I'll wink my eye when she comes back so you can jump out and yell surprise, okay?" he whispered to me from the side of his mouth.

I was paralyzed.

Hearing her return to the door, I looked at the delivery man and saw him wink his left eye. When I saw her hand snake out of the door to pay for the food, I stepped out to look at her face to face. I was already crying uncontrollably when I saw a tall, statuesque woman before me, wearing nothing but the same Harvard Medical t-shirt that I had worn almost a year ago to the day.

FIVE

Ten years later, I found myself trying to remember the details of the girl's face. I couldn't remember whether she was prettier than me or not. The only thing I could remember was the shirt that she was wearing and the smirk that came across her lips when she saw me, as if she knew exactly who I was.

When I stepped through the doorway of Gabe's apartment, a part of me died. After that night, I would never again believe in the naïve idea of a perfect, all-consuming love. In the years that followed, I recognized that even if I forgave him for what he had done, I would never be able to forgive him for taking that part of me away.

Over a decade later, it was hard to imagine that I had punched the girl in her face. Riding in the back of the ambulance, I cringed thinking about how I had used Gabe's golf clubs to destroy the one thing that I could find in his apartment that meant something to him, his bike, Lamborghini.

When I saw it leaning on his bookcase, it stood as a reminder of the first night we spent together and everything that I thought I loved about him. Enraged, I demolished the bike as he watched in horror from across his living room. He didn't move and didn't attempt to stop me. He only whispered, "Lotus, I'm so sorry," as I swung his nine iron, wedge and driver at his bike until each one broke. Once I was finally exhausted, I walked past him and the girl sitting on the floor whimpering, attempted to stanch her bloody nose. Without looking at either of them, I dropped the driver at the door before picking up my purse and leaving.

It wasn't until I was a block away that I heard his voice calling after me. Fueled by a combination of anger, hurt, and sadness, I ran faster than I ever had in my life. Each time my foot pounded the pavement, I felt a little better and a little worse. When I finally got to a cab, I jumped in and begged the driver to accelerate. Looking out the back window as the cab drive off, I could see Gabe still running after me. He wasn't wearing a coat or any shoes. Tearfully, I watched him until he disappeared from my view as the cab turned a corner.

I flew home to Chicago that night. My parents didn't ask any questions when I showed up on their doorstep in the middle of the night with bloodshot eyes. As hurt as I was, I felt like an idiot because deep down I still wanted to be with him. There wasn't anything he could have said to change anything, but every day I hoped that he would call. I still wanted him to fight for me like I had been willing to fight for him.

I waited for some form of communication from him, but for almost a week but there was nothing. It wasn't until Christmas Eve that he left a letter and a package for me on my parents' porch.

I took the package inside and opened it on the floor of the foyer. Before I looked inside the box, I read the typed letter that was taped to the top.

Lotus,

A year ago when you fell asleep in my arms, I realized that you were the person I wanted to spend my life with. I was certain of the role I wanted for you to have in my life. For a long time, I felt both lucky and screwed to have fallen in love with you considering that we only had a short time remaining to be together.

Since that day, I have continued to love you. That simple fact never has and will never change, regardless of the mistakes that I have made. However, because I have hurt you, and you are the one person who means more to me than anything, I know that you deserve better than I can give you.

The people who are responsible for making me who I am no longer love each other. I don't know what to make of that. While I want to beg you to forgive me, the truth is that right

now I will only hurt you more than I already have.

I love you. Know that any other woman will simply be a placeholder for a space that only you can fill. That fact will never change - regardless of the space or the time that we find ourselves in.

I love you, and this belongs to you,

Gabe

Wiping off tears, I opened the box to see his Harvard Medical School t-shirt inside.

SIX

Looking around the emergency room, I remembered exactly why I hated Lakeside Memorial as much as I did. There was a girl throwing up into a biohazard bag to my left and a toddler with his mother coughing violently to my right. A drunken homeless man was lying across three chairs in front of me, and there was a steady procession of EMTs, police officers, and drug addicts in and out of the ER's rotating doors.

As I sat in a corner of the cold air-filled lobby by myself, I waited to be called by one of the triage nurses. Sitting there alone, I reminded myself that I couldn't be upset at Nick for not coming; there was no way for him to know the real reason I needed him with me.

I tried to not think about the last time I was at the hospital, five years earlier, just after Nick and I had started dating. The decor hadn't changed much except for the chairs that now lined the perimeter of the room and the improved choices for candy that filled the vending machines.

The same pale pink paint masked the walls. The room's bright florescent lights still made everyone look like zombies. The same Jamaican woman sat near the front door to check people in, calling everyone who entered "honey," "child," "gal," or "sweetie." When she spied me, I saw a hint of recognition in her face but I walked past her quickly and hoped to God that she hadn't made the connection.

After being called into Triage for an initial assessment, I returned to my seat and tried to distract myself. Looking out the window, I could see snow falling in big slow flakes on the streets outside the hospital. The blanket of white that covered everything made it appear as if the world had come to a standstill. The way the snow covered the Gothic university buildings quickly took my mind back five years.

I had paced the emergency room for hours, praying that my little sister Layla would be okay. Once I was finally allowed to see her, I walked numbly through the long hallway to the room where she lay unconscious. With every step that I took, I could only muster the strength to say, "I'm so sorry, Layla," to myself, hoping that somehow she could hear me.

I was trying to make sense of the news that the doctors had just given my family. I was oblivious to everything around me until I heard my name.

It had been five years since I had seen him, but I could never forget the sound of his voice. When I looked up and saw Gabe standing in front of me, I froze.

Looking towards the room where Layla lay, he continued to move towards me. "I'm a resident here and I saw your sister's name on the docket. I thought it was a bad coincidence until I saw Lola. I was on my way to speak with the trauma surgeon on her case."

Seeing him and having to accept that I would never hear Layla's laugh again felt like too much to bear. Without acknowledging what he had said, I walked past him until I was in the doorway of her room. Standing behind the open curtains, I looked at her and tried to take in every feature of her face. My parents sat silently on each side of her bed, unaware of my presence.

"She had just returned to her dorm room from a run when the aneurysm ruptured," I said without looking at him. "The bleeding was too severe and it caused irreversible damage. She will never wake up."

As the words were leaving my mouth, my legs collapsed. Gabe picked me up and took me into a small room where we sat for an hour. He said nothing; he only held me while I cried. At that moment, our past no longer mattered. I was only grateful that he was there.

Once I finally had the strength to stand up, he held onto my hands.

"I love you," he uttered, looking down at the floor. "I'm sorry if I shouldn't have said that. I just want you to know that I'm here if you need me."

It wasn't the reaction I imagined that I would have once I saw him again, but I didn't have the ability to lie.

"I know you do," I said, walking to the door. Without looking back at him, I said, "I love you, too."

I didn't see him again until Layla's funeral a week later. I never attempted to contact him after that. I was in too much grief to unpack the emotions of our past, and as the months went by, it began to seem pointless. As time passed, I had no idea if he still worked at Lakeshore Memorial Hospital. Before today, I had never wanted to know.

Unnerved by the memories, I began to gather my things to leave. Just as I walked past the Jamaican lady by the door, my name was called. My stomach tightened, and I stopped in my tracks. I turned around to face him after taking a deep breath.

He was just as I remembered.

When I looked at him, I could see the look of concern in his dark grey eyes. Though his eyebrows were furrowed, he forced himself to smile. It wasn't until I saw the title, **Dr. Gabriel Lincoln, Attending Emergency Room Physician**, on his doctor's coat that I smiled back.

I should have walked to him, but my shoes felt glued to the floor. Observing my lack of response, the Jamaican receptionist chimed in. "I *tink* he wants you to go with him, sweet gal," she said tauntingly as if she knew the lurid details of our past.

As I took a step in his direction, I could feel his eyes piercing me. Though the room was crowded and noisy, I felt like I was a young girl back in his apartment - trying my best to not appear nervous. My eyes took stock of the ways in which he had changed, but I was surprised at how much he looked the same. His face, his smile, even his coy demeanor were just as I recalled.

When I finally got the nerve to look in his eyes, I caught him looking down at my wedding ring. I opened my mouth to greet him, but he spoke instead.

"Lotus, what are you doing here?" he asked bluntly.

He turned to lead me through a pair of double doors before I had time to respond. "I didn't get a chance to review your patient notes yet but come on and follow me to the back."

Walking behind him, I tried to think of something to say that would break the ice.

"Don't worry, it's not an aneurysm," I said. I regretted the comment as soon as it came out of my mouth.

His head lifted from the iPad he was scanning and his long gait immediately stopped short. He couldn't hide his annoyance.

"Why would you joke like that? Your file says that you fainted in your house after running. With your family's medical history, I would think that you would be more concerned."

His judgmental tone immediately made me feel defensive.

"It was a stupid thing to say, but I'm trying my best not to freak out being back here. I spent the last five years trying to block this hospital and..." I hesitated, stopping short of finishing my thought.

"And what?" he asked before opening the curtain to my examination room.

"I just didn't know if you still worked here," I trailed off, stepping past him to enter the room.

After closing the curtain behind us, he sat in a chair across from the bed where he directed me to sit. Suddenly, his rigid demeanor softened.

"I'm sorry that it has been so long."

Immediately feeling uncomfortable, I tried to redirect the conversation.

"It's been a long time, but I'm glad to see that you are doing well. How are your sisters?"

He sat back in his chair and stared at me. "Lotus, I'm trying to say that I'm sorry for not calling after everything happened with Layla. I should have called, but I didn't, and I want you to know that I am sorry for that."

"Gabe, it's fine," I said, annoyed. "I can barely remember anything from that entire year. I made it through, and that's what is important. There wasn't anything for you to say or do."

He leaned forward to speak, but I wouldn't let him.

"Gabe, don't."

The tension that I thought had begun to ease had obviously returned. I was surprised to see a glimpse of hurt in his eyes just as the curtains opened behind him, and a nurse appeared. With slumped shoulders, I wondered why the woman looked so tired even though I overheard her say that she had just begun her shift. The soft features of her round face seemed unnaturally hardened by the bags that surrounded her eyes. Briefly distracted by how much she reminded me of my first-grade teacher, I watched her as she set up a phlebotomy kit and specimen containers on the counter across from me. When she turned around and smiled at me, her dimples made me instantly feel more comfortable.

Not wanting to be left alone with Gabe, I hoped that she would stay in the room with us. My eyes quietly pleaded for her not to leave as she politely introduced herself. Obviously feeling uncomfortable by my intense staring, she shifted her eyes to Gabe as he briefed her on the information that I had provided to the triage nurse and listened carefully as he began to order what sounded like a long succession of tests.

On her way out of the room, the nurse stopped and turned towards me. "You popped up in our system under a different last name. Are you recently married?"

"Yes, she's married," he answered for me as he turned his back from us and began to wash his hands.

"Great," the nurse said, flashing him a curious look. "I'll update your records now. I'll be back with a cup so we can run a urinalysis first."

Pausing briefly from signing the remaining medical orders, he searched my face for a response. He then nodded to the nurse that he didn't need anything else. When the curtains were closed, he continued where he had left off.

"I know that I should have called you."

I lifted my hand in the air to signal that I wanted him to stop. "Why are you doing this?"

"I know that you're married, but I feel like I owe you an explanation. I didn't call you because I couldn't run the risk of causing you any additional pain, especially not then. Every time I convinced myself to call, I thought of five more reasons not to. I don't want you to think that I didn't care. You were all I thought about for months."

I fought the urge to feel anything about the things that he said. I was hurt, irritated, and angry that he chose to purge his emotions without any real consideration of how they might affect me. My mind told me to be appreciative of his words, but I couldn't since they only served the purpose of making him feel better about his actions. A part of me hated him as I watched from across the room. Another part of me, a part of me that I was afraid to admit still existed, wanted to hear what he had to say.

He kept his distance in the small room as he continued to talk.

"I have always wanted nothing more than for you to be happy. But after Boston..."

"When you cheated on me," I interrupted.

He paused and looked down before continuing.

"...and after Layla died, I knew that it was best for me to stay at a distance. I don't know if it was the right decision. I spent a long time regretting it. But it was one that I was willing to live with – even if I knew that it would make me physically ill to see you with someone else."

I began to gather my things. I cursed Nick for not being there with me and tried to focus my thoughts on the life that we were building together. If I allowed myself to think of anything else – Gabe's words, our past, how I once felt about him – who knows what I might say.

As I reached for my coat, Gabe walked towards me.

"Lotus, I'm sorry. I didn't wake up this morning and expect to see you when I came to work. If you hadn't come into the emergency room, I would have continued to stay as far away from you as possible. But you are here, in my emergency room, and you need to be seen. If I've made you uncomfortable, then I will have another doctor put on your case. I recognize that everything that I just said to you was more for me than it was for you. It was selfish and for that reason, I'm sorry."

He grabbed my coat out of my hand and returned it to the hook on the wall. As he touched my hand, I instantly felt vulnerable. I couldn't let go.

As if he sensed that I was defenseless, he pulled me into his arms. Every tear that I had refused to cry and every ounce of sadness I had buried poured out of me. Every thought that told me to hate or forget him was silent. I let go of trying to feel anything but what I felt.

With my head buried in his chest, I felt the brush of his lips on my forehead. It was maybe a few seconds, but it felt a lot longer than that — enough time for me to remember our most intimate moments, the carefreeness of the love that we had, my youthful confidence. We were both jolted back into the present moment when we heard a knock on the glass sliding door. Stepping away from him, I wiped my eyes before the nurse reappeared in the room with a sterile cup in her hand.

"Here you go, sweetie. The restroom is two doors to the left. Remember, wipe, pee, wipe, and seal the cup. Bring it back with you in the room, and we will go from there. Doctor, you are needed in another room," she said, looking uncomfortably at both of us before she quickly disappeared behind the curtain again.

"Promise me you won't leave before I come back," Gabriel said.

"I won't," I responded without looking up at him. I didn't know why I felt embarrassed.

I followed him out of the room, and we headed in two different directions. Several minutes later, I returned to the room alone, trying to manage the torrent of thoughts that flooded my mind.

Sitting on the edge of the bed, I made myself think of Mexico. I closed my eyes and envisioned Nick's face and how I felt falling asleep next to him every night. I thought about how he would feel if he knew I was here with Gabe, whom I only briefly told him about many years ago. Guilt washed over me. Though I had done nothing wrong, it still felt like there was something that I needed to confess.

I was still sorting through my thoughts when I heard the sliding door open again. When I sat up on the bed, I was surprised to see a smiling, short and chubby, middle-aged man I didn't recognize standing before me.

"Hi, Lotus. I'm Dr. Blackmon. I'll be taking over your case. Dr. Lincoln gave me the results of your urinalysis. Let me be the first to congratulate you. You are pregnant."

SEVEN

When the cab pulled in front of my office building, I saw the executive director standing outside smoking a cigarette. Though it was Friday and I had the option of working from home, going into the office would be a welcome distraction. Praying that I could slip into the building without his noticing me, I pulled the hood of my parka over my head before getting out. With sunglasses covering my eyes, I hurried past him as quickly as I could. Just as my hand gripped the knob of the building's door, I heard him calling my name.

"Lotus, you DO know that I can see you, right?" he asked while taking another pull on his cigarette. "Didn't your email say that you were in the hospital or something?"

When I turned to face him, he was peering down at me over his glasses with a thinly veiled look of irritation.

"But since you are here, I need you to finish a grant application that is due on Monday."

I took a deep cleansing breath because I knew what he was going to say next. I stood listlessly waiting for the litany of orders that were going to follow as soon as he caught his breath.

"I also need the agenda for next month's Board of Directors meeting and for you to make a few presentation slides for my meeting with the deputy mayor. I've also been thinking that we need to start a mentoring program for high school students. Let's call it 'A Passport to Citizenship,'" he said as he waved his two hands across his face as if he were reading the name on a Broadway marquee.

I stared at him blankly. Praying that he was done and desperate to get inside to my office, I reached again for the handle of the door. As I took a step into the lobby, I heard him call my name again.

"Lotus, one more thing. Start thinking about what we can do about teen pregnancy rates."

For a fleeting moment, I wanted to ask if he was serious but I unfortunately already knew that he was. Asking me to "think" about teen pregnancy rates was as random and broad as asking someone to "think" about AIDS in Africa. There was no point in asking a follow-up question because I suspected that he wouldn't have a logical response. We both knew that he only needed talking points to add to his campaign website. Rather than show my aggravation, I nodded to acknowledge that I heard his request before finally heading through the doors.

Once in my office, I closed the door and sat down at my desk without taking off my coat. I kept hearing Gabe's voice in my head, asking me not to leave. I hated how helpless I felt with him, and how vulnerable and exposed I remembered feeling when we were together. Even after ten years, the fact that the feeling remained was something that I wasn't ready to acknowledge.

I usually dreaded being in the small room but today my office felt like my only refuge. I had considered going home, but thinking about Gabe in the home that I shared with my husband felt like a betrayal. Unable to focus on any one thought, I turned to the only thing sitting on my desk other than my computer, a framed picture of Lola, Layla and me. Along the bottom of the frame were three engraved words: Amor est Aeterna.

It was our last picture together. It was taken only a few weeks before Layla died, during a family vacation to Hawaii.

It was a trip we took every year since we were kids and as adults it was the only time that we got to see our extended family outside of the holidays. For two weeks, twenty-five of my aunts, uncles, and cousins rented four houses near the Lahaina Harbor. Besides drinking endless Mai Tais and margaritas, it also came to be one of the few times I could anticipate time alone with my sisters. The day before we were to leave, my oldest cousin Dakota chartered a sailboat to cruise between Mau'i and Lana'i for one last day of snorkeling. While everyone else was in the water, Layla and I volunteered to stay on the deck to look out for whales when the truth is that we wanted to stay on the deck to talk.

"Do you ever regret not going to law school in Boston?" Layla asked out of nowhere.

We had been talking about Nick, whom I had just begun to date when she interrupted me with her question. I had just told her that this *new guy* was the first person that I liked since Gabe, so her question caught me completely off guard.

"No, I don't regret not going, at least not at this point in my life. Obviously, it would have been a bad mistake," I replied without putting any real thought into her question.

I sat in silence for a moment and continued, "Things happen the way they're supposed to happen, ya' know? At least I hope they do. What made you ask me that question?"

"I don't know, Lo," she said coyly, covering her eyes from the bright sun.

I was bothered that she brought it up, but I was also curious as to what made her think of Gabe, especially since his name hadn't come up between us in years.

"Layla, seriously? Why did you ask me that?" I continued to press until she gave me an honest response.

Though she was four years younger than me, I valued her opinion. She always displayed a level of clarity and wisdom that I envied.

"Lotus, I love you. No one wants you to be happier than I do, except for Mom and Dad and maybe Lola. It's just that...I don't know," she trailed off again, looking out towards the water.

"Layla, I am going to choke you if you don't just say it."

She laughed, "I had never seen you as happy as you were with Gabe. In all the years that have passed and considering all the guys that you have dated since, I wonder if you are happy. You tend to play it safe when it comes to your heart and you don't have to do that. Love has always been and will always be a gamble. We just have to trust that it's a gamble worth making."

We sat quietly for a few minutes as I thought about what she had just said.

"But what does that have to do with Gabe's asking me to move to Boston?" I asked.

"Look, I understood why you didn't go. You all had talked about it before you went to London and then he screwed up. I just remember that when you told me that he asked you to move to Boston after graduation, I was excited for you. I prayed that you would decide to go even after everything happened. I always imagined that you all would bump into each other in Copley Square and realize that fate had brought you back into each other's lives," she said, laughing.

"Copley Square? That's hilarious. I can't believe you never told me this before. Why are you telling me now?" I asked her.

"There was something about the way you were with him that made me want that for myself. A part of me will always secretly root for him because of how happy he made you. I guess I wonder if, despite everything that happened between the two of you, whether you could see yourself back with him if the opportunity presented itself?"

"If the opportunity presented itself?" I asked with a laugh. "I highly doubt if I'll ever see Gabriel again, Layla. It's a sweet sentiment, but I think we both have probably moved on."

"Amor est aeterna," she said, smiling, as she looked back towards the open water.

"Amor est aeterna? You are such a nerd. What does that mean, my little linguist?" I asked as I leaned over and gave her a hug.

She hugged me back and kissed my cheek. "It's Latin, sis. It means that love is eternal."

As I stared at the picture with the words written underneath, I could hear her voice as clearly as if she were standing next to me.

"You could have given me a little warning," I said aloud, believing that somewhere she sat observing the entire fiasco.

I wished she were there to help me sort through my thoughts, to help me figure out what it meant that I ran into him. I would have asked her if she had a feeling all those years ago that Gabe's paths and my would collide again. Knowing that was impossible, the loneliness I felt in my office burrowed deeper than usual; I became angry with her all over again for dying and angry with Gabe for saying everything that he said.

I grabbed my journal out of my purse. Staring at it, I prayed that the flurry of thoughts in my mind would suddenly organize themselves on the pages in front of me. Just as I felt ready to write, my cell phone vibrated on the desk. Glancing down at it I saw that Nick had texted me several times over the past few hours.

His last text read, **Haven't heard from you and I'm getting a little worried. Please call me. I have something to tell you.**

I still wanted to be upset at him, but my guilt made it impossible. The part of me that wished that he had come with me to the hospital flinched at the idea of his meeting Gabe without forewarning. It seemed like the hand of fate that steered me to seeing Gabe was the same hand that made sure that Nick wasn't there.

Rationally, I knew that I couldn't hold Nick responsible for what I was feeling, but I counted his absence as one of the many ways he had changed since we married. The romance and friendship of our courtship had been quickly exchanged for the pragmatism and practicalities of marriage. Weekly date nights soon played a distant second to planning for our future by way of his professional goals. Too often, making time for each other became a scheduled event rather than something that we did naturally. I often joked that I was a glorified roommate with sexual benefits.

After a few minutes, I decided not to ignore his texts any longer. I responded:

Not dead. Came to work for a few hours. Meet you at home for taco night. I will pick up the tequila.

I turned my chair to look out the window after sending the message. Though I had been here for nearly an hour, I could still see the executive director on the streets below chain-smoking. Seeing him spending half the day on a smoking break would have typically irritated me, but today he could have stayed out there all night. For once, my thoughts were no more focused on being here than his were. I could only think about the reality that I was going to become a mother, the various possibilities of how my husband would react to the news, and the fact that, as much as I tried, I couldn't get the smell of Gabe's cologne out of my mind.

EIGHT

When I got off the elevator, I could hear the soft hum of jazz coming from my condo. The smell of garlic and cheese filled the hallway, and as I neared the door of my home I was stunned to realize that it was coming from our unit.

Surprised that Nick beat me home for once, I didn't know what to do with the balloons, cake, tequila, and bag of tacos that were in my hands. Still unsure of exactly how I was going to tell Nick that I was pregnant, I reluctantly left the cake and balloons outside our door until I could figure out how to sneak them into the house undetected.

As I walked into the kitchen, I saw fresh white tulips and an opened bottle of red wine sitting on the table. On the stove was my favorite dish, lobster and shrimp fettuccine, next to a fresh loaf of garlic bread and a tossed salad on the counter. Seeing that

Nick was obviously in a good mood, I became less anxious about our impending conversation.

I looked around the unit, but he was nowhere to be found. I started to think that he had gone out for a minute just as a draft of cold air blew through our bedroom door into the hallway. When I glanced for a second time through the open door, I saw him standing on the balcony smoking a cigar, looking over the frozen lake below.

His back was still turned to me as I stepped out onto the balcony. I wrapped my arms around him as tightly as possible and dug my face into the softness of his dark blue cashmere sweater. Though the smell of his cigar was overpowering, I also picked up the spicy scent of his hair and skin, and I wrapped my arms around him even more tightly. It was the first time I'd felt relaxed all day.

Nick pulled my hands up to his mouth and gently kissed them. When he turned around to look at me, I knew he was going to let me have it.

"Should I assume that taco night is cancelled?" I asked with a wry smile.

"Why didn't you call me?" he asked, ignoring my question.

"I knew you were in class and I had a lot of work to get through once I got into the office. The doctor said that, *for the most part*, I'm perfectly fine. My blood pressure was a little low, so that's why I passed out," I replied, stepping away from him.

I took another step back into our bedroom. "I'm cold so I'm about to go eat," I said, hoping my response would suffice. I took a few steps and turned to see whether he was following me or not, but he hadn't moved from the deck.

"*For the most part?*" he asked.

"Yes, Nick. I'm fine, I promise. Can you please come inside and close the door? It's very cold out there," I persisted.

Reluctantly, he followed me into the kitchen, where he sat at the counter as I fixed my plate. Even with my back to him, I felt him studying my every move. I had the feeling that he was either waiting to say something or waiting to ask me something.

"So what's up with you? Jazz? Lobster Fettuccine? Cigars? Are we happy or sad or did you look at *The Lion King* again while I was at work?"

He smiled, but he didn't laugh.

His thick eyebrows remained pensive as I sat at the counter across from him. I began to chuck forkfuls of pasta down my throat to keep myself from having to make small talk until I was ready to tell him everything. I had rehearsed what I wanted to say to him at least a hundred times but I still had to resist the urge to blurt out, "I'm having a baby" just to get it off of my chest.

When he poured himself a full glass of Shiraz, I realized that he was just as nervous as I was. I started to fear the worst just as he began to speak.

"After my last final, the department chair called a faculty meeting to discuss the spring lecture series, as well as upcoming research projects. When it was over, he invited us to his office for a glass of champagne. It caught us all off guard because he doesn't drink."

He paused to take another long sip of wine. It was obvious that he was choosing his words carefully.

"And once we were all in his office, he announced that he was sad to announce that someone in the department would be leaving next fall..."

A sinking feeling came to my stomach as I reached across the table and took a small sip of his wine, despite the fact that I knew I shouldn't. I knew what was about to happen and that there was nothing I could do to stop it. I felt suspended in time. I imagined this was exactly how the survivors of the Titanic felt.

A wide grin came across his face.

"The Chair asked me to stand next to him in the middle of the room. I honestly had no idea what was going on because I didn't expect to hear back about my research this soon. Seconds later, he announced that he received word that I was awarded the fellowship. Lotus, I will be teaching in Paris, at the Sorbonne next fall."

Though music continued to play, the room grew deathly silent. His gaze never broke from mine as I calculated the best reaction for the moment.

"I'm so proud of you, baby," I said, forcing myself to look happy. I got up from my chair and gave him a hug.

"You have worked so hard for this, Nick. No one deserves this more than you."

He stood and embraced me for so long that I could feel the emotion that he couldn't communicate at that moment. Slowly, his arms moved from my shoulders to my waist as he lifted me onto our granite counter before kissing me.

"This is what we have dreamed about, Lo. We can leave for Paris this summer," he said as he continued to kiss me in between his words.

"We can start looking for apartments in the 5th Arrondissement by the school."

He pulled my hair back and began to kiss my neck. I forgot about being pregnant, and I forgot about seeing Gabe. I just wanted to be there with him at that moment. I began to unbutton his shirt when we were both startled by the sound of pounding on the door.

I jumped off the counter as Nick made his way down the hallway. It wasn't until I heard the sound of the building manager's voice that I cursed aloud. My heart pounded profusely as I sat, trying to listen to their exchange. A minute later, the door closed, and I could hear Nick slowly walk down the hallway until he reappeared holding the bouquet of balloons and the half-melted ice cream cake that I had picked up on my way home.

With his shirt still unbuttoned, he stood across the room with a look of confusion. I knew he was waiting for me to give him an explanation. Realizing that this was the moment of truth, I lowered myself from the counter and picked up his glass of wine. I handed it to him and said, "Nick, I'm pregnant."

NINE

Their faces were frozen in shock.

Lola had stopped chopping onions on her cutting board, and my cousin Dakota hadn't sipped her mocha for at least five minutes. With the exception of the voices of the kids playing in the yard and the hum of the enormous refrigerator, my sister's house was silent as I recounted each detail of the day, almost four weeks ago, when I first learned that I was pregnant. When I concluded the story with Nick's revelation about Paris, both of their mouths dropped open in disbelief.

"I can't believe that you would wait this long to tell us this story!" Dakota yelled as she kicked me with her riding boots underneath the table covered with kid-friendly condiments, packets of organic brown sugar and an out-of-place tiny, jointed action figure. "I swear I always knew Gabe was going to pop back up sooner than later. I'm just surprised it took this long.

Lola and I had a secret bet last year that he was going to burst through the chapel doors and try to stop the wedding, singing Adele's "Someone Like You.'"

We hadn't met for our monthly brunch since Christmas because no one felt like driving through the snow to Lola's house in Evanston. Though her Colonial-style home with its big, sensibly furnished rooms, redwood deck and Weber grill was a welcoming location for summer barbeques and swim parties, its location on top of a hill made it a death trap to visit during the winter. By the third blizzard of the season, the three of us agreed to postpone our next gathering until the mounds of snow and ice covering her long driveway began to melt. Finally, by the beginning of February, when the ponds around her home had begun to melt, Dakota and I decided that it was time for us to make the drive back to the north shore.

"I hate Gabe, but I do love that song," Lola said, rolling her eyes from the other side of the granite-topped kitchen island.

"As soon as I saw tears in those big brown eyes I knew that it had something to do with Gabe. I didn't know why, but I knew that somehow he had slithered his way into your mind on the day of your wedding," she said without looking at me as she began to pull vegetables from her refrigerator.

Her normally soft features had been distorted into a frown since the second she heard Gabe's name. She had despised him for over a decade since we had broken up. I knew that a discussion focused on him would go nowhere, so I tried to change the subject.

"That's hilarious, but I'm sure you would have tackled him at the door," I replied sarcastically before stuffing my mouth with a fork full of the crepes that she made earlier. "But in the bigger scheme of things, this isn't about Gabe. In fact, I would appreciate it if we didn't even talk about him because, in my mind, seeing him was an awful coincidence. My problem right now is figuring out what to do about Paris."

Dakota stood from the table and walked to the refrigerator to pour herself another mimosa from the pitcher. After taking a drink, she looked back towards me and said, "Paris isn't a problem, Lotus. It's an opportunity of a lifetime. On the other hand, I can tell you about problems."

In the brief pause as she took another sip, I looked at my sister from across the kitchen. She flashed me a look of warning before putting her chopping knife on the counter and taking a long exaggerated gulp of her own Bellini. We both tried to keep ourselves from laughing because I had just put my foot in my mouth.

"You want to know problems?" Dakota asked, standing in the middle of the room. "Problems were when every man that you meet wants to become a music producer, an actor, or a party promoter. Problems are when you're on the phone with a guy that you are starting to like, and he recounts a memory of you and him together that NEVER took place. Problems are when you broke up with someone almost a year ago, but he continues to send you pictures of himself, *every single morning*, staring at his camera phone like a damn psycho!"

Lola and I burst into laughter. Though she could easily have been mistaken for a model, Dakota did have horrible luck when it came to relationships. After graduating at the top of her class from Wharton, she took a job at a top venture capital fund in New York. Her drive and assertiveness intimidated most men until she met her match with Louis Sterling, a tech entrepreneur whose company had become a client of her firm. After six months of what she often described as a "Sex and the City" meets "Jagged Edge" love affair, he informed her over dinner one night that he had a wife and two children who lived in Connecticut. Devastated and paranoid that her professional reputation had been ruined, she moved back to Chicago and opened up her own boutique investment firm, swearing off any men who were just as accomplished or who made more money than she.

"It's not funny!" she said as she gulped down her second glass of a Bellini. "I have been professionally successful; I make a lot of money, and I'm in the gym five days a week to keep my tits from touching my knees. The only guys I meet want me to finance their damn childhood pipe dreams! Then you have Lotus who has Nick, the most dedicated and ambitious man on the face of this Earth, and Gabe, the most beautiful and emotionally fragile doctor known to man, who continues to come back from the dead every five years like a damn cicada. I'm just saying that those aren't problems. You have two men pining for your love, and that's not a bad position to be in."

I looked at Lola for help. Once Dakota started talking about her dating life, there was no coming back. We both knew it was only a matter of time before she brought up Louis and if that happened, the rest of our morning would be filled with our planning various scenarios on how to murder him without being caught.

"You want to know problems?" Lola asked as she finally sat at the table with us to eat.

It was hard to imagine what she could say, considering that her husband, Michael, had just been nominated as 'Volunteer of the Year' at their children's school PTA and was undeniably the friendliest guy anyone would ever meet.

"Problems are when your husband is too cheap to hire a real painter, so he finds a random person standing outside of a home improvement store and asks him if he wants a job repainting your kitchen. Imagine walking into your house and finding a drug addict painting your kitchen walls because your husband doesn't want to pay full price for a professional paint job."

She was exaggerating, but now she was in her zone. "Problems are when your husband thinks that foreplay is saying, 'Hop on the sausage.' Problems are when you have to hide in the bathroom just to get a quiet moment away from your kids," she said boastfully as if she had just won some type of competition.

I shook my head at her from across the table.

"Nice try, Lola, but stop calling that poor man a drug addict. He was just an undocumented worker with diabetes. I told you that when you called and asked me to Google the name of the drug valve that you found in the garbage can. It was insulin. Not crack. Leave Michael alone. He's perfect and the best accountant in the world so you can't divorce him, even if you wanted to. Besides, the kitchen's beautiful," I said motioning towards the soft pale yellow walls, which set off the brick-colored tile floor. With the granite counters and maple table, the whole room had an earthy feeling that always made me hungry.

"He COULD have been a crack-head and you are obviously missing my point. My point is that real problems involve things that you can't control. I love my husband and, yes, he is the kindest person that I know. He is also cheap. Nevertheless, we have two kids, two dogs, a bird and a damn goldfish together so I'm stuck with him and his cheap ways and bad foreplay..."

Her tone grew more serious as she continued, "...but our marriage isn't easy. We are just committed to making it work, even during the times when we might not want to. So I agree that your real problem isn't Gabe. Don't allow yourself to revisit those feelings unless you think there is a purpose in doing so. Your real problem is figuring out how to build a marriage and family that works for both of you and Nick...whether you are raising your child in Paris or not. You can't be angry at the type of life Nick is trying to build for your family when you are making yourself sit on the sidelines."

She paused for a moment before continuing. From the moment I first mentioned Gabe's name I knew she had been gauging my reaction to seeing him. I knew that she had been waiting to ask me something. After we had finished the remainder of our breakfasts in silence, I waited for her to say whatever it was that she had to say.

Finally, Lola's eyes narrowed in my direction.

"Lotus, what I've been trying to understand is this. We talk a few times a week, but you managed to keep all of this from me for almost a month. You know that isn't normal, right?

Why - no - *how* could you wait so long before telling either of us what has been going on with you?"

She was sitting in front of me, and Dakota was sitting beside me. Their judging eyes were burning holes into my head. Before I arrived, I anticipated that they would feel slightly betrayed that I had kept so much from them. I hoped that they would understand that seeing Gabe was something that I simply wanted to forget. Embarrassed, I shook my head and looked down at my empty plate.

"I've been processing things. I guess I felt like if I talked about it then I was betraying Nick for some reason. If I can be totally honest, I just wanted to forget about it," I confessed.

"So you were going to act like it didn't happen?" she asked in a disapproving tone.

She was implying something, but it was unclear to me what she was trying to suggest. Tired of her beating around the bush, I just wanted her to say whatever it was that she had to say.

"What are you trying to get at?" I asked.

"I'm not trying to get at anything, Lotus," she said, instantly softening her voice. "I'm just asking whether you would have acknowledged anything about seeing Gabe if we hadn't gotten together today. I mean, even to *yourself?* Or would you have compartmentalized seeing him and your feelings around that like you do to everything else that's hurtful? Look, you know I am not a big fan of Gabe and that I think he is a major prick.

However, I don't think that avoidance is the answer either. You spend so much time trying to fix other people's issues, and then you sweep your shit under the carpet. I'm just afraid that it was going to come back and bite you one day."

She was right. Instead of trying to refute anything, I considered everything that she said while also trying to think of excuses to leave. I was grateful to Dakota for finally breaking the silence.

"Is it possible for Nick to defer the fellowship for a year?" she asked.

"I asked him if that was a possibility, but apparently there is no guarantee that the position will be available in a year," I told them.

The guilt that I felt thinking of the possibility of Nick losing his fellowship was crushing. I hesitated to tell Lola and Dakota that we hadn't slept in the same bed more than three times since I told him that I was pregnant. I knew they would think that I was irrational, but everything about my relationship with him seemed to change the moment I told him that we were having a baby. His typically laidback demeanor felt cold and distant, his impassiveness felt detached.

"I feel like Nick resents me," I blurted out. "My biggest fear is that even if he ends up becoming the best father in the world, if he doesn't take this fellowship he may always look at me and the baby as the stumbling blocks to what could have been the opportunity of his career."

I began to ramble through my various contingency plans. "I've been looking into programs at the Sorbonne that support fellows from abroad and their families and I realized that it's doable. There is a university-sponsored nanny-share program and everything. Even though we agreed that we wouldn't decide anything until spring, I'm going to push him to accept the offer. It's not the ideal solution, but I feel like it's the best decision. He said that he is willing to forgo the fellowship all together if he has to, but I'm not willing to allow him to do that."

Reaching across the table, Lola took hold of my hand.

"Lo, it's noble that you are willing to fall on the sword, but shouldn't you respect that Nick is willing to wait a year if he thinks it's the best decision? If he is willing to roll the dice and wait until next year then why would you try to convince him otherwise?"

Though Lola and Dakota were my family, they were also my two closest friends. There were things about my marriage that I was afraid to admit to them out of fear of what they would think. I learned while dating in college that there was always a line that shouldn't be crossed when it came to sharing details about my relationships, even with them. Once I gave them a reason to either love or dislike someone, there was usually no going back. As we sat around Lola's kitchen counter, I struggled with finding the line that separated the private effects of my marriage and the emotions that I needed to get off my chest.

I looked at Lola and finally admitted my biggest fear. "I'm going to force him to take it because he's been unhappy since I told him I was pregnant, and I feel like he will grow even unhappier if we don't do this."

The looks on their faces were exactly what I had wanted to avoid. I feared that out of their love for me they would look at Nick differently, which was not what I wanted.

"Do you mean he is anxious or do you think he is truly unhappy?" Dakota asked with worried eyes.

"Both, perhaps? He's always stressed out. We rarely have sex anymore. He's been completely uninterested in the pregnancy."

"Lotus, I don't want you to freak out because Nick's not having the reaction that you've seen in romantic comedies about your pregnancy. Most men don't develop a real connection with their children until they are born and can see them with their own two eyes. Even then, most men don't like babies. Even Michael, 'Daddy of the Year' - didn't step into fatherhood until the kids were talking, walking and could tell him exactly what it was that they needed. Before then, he could probably be best described as a great babysitter."

Her words made me feel slightly better. "But it seemed like Dad was always present. I feel like, no matter what, he has always been a reassuring figure, always lurking somewhere in the background to save the day. Even when we did something wrong, we knew he would always be there to help. I never felt like he was too distracted to be our dad."

"That's because Dad had already figured out the fathering thing by the time you came along. I'm pretty sure I thought Dad was either mute or deaf until I was five, so I remember deferring to Mom for everything. I'm pretty sure the first thing he ever said to me was on my first day of kindergarten when he asked, 'Do you need lunch money?' Before you came, Daddy just went to work, watched ESPN, and played with wood in the garage until it was time to go to sleep.

She walked around the table and gave me a hug. "Don't worry, sweetie, Nick will come around. I'm sure of it."

"I hope you are right," I said with a half-smile. "But for the record, Daddy did drop us off at school every day and at least he would try to braid our hair when Mom was out of town for conferences."

"That's true but that was after years of Mom's training him on how to be a father and threatening to leave him if he didn't figure it out," she said with a laugh.

Dakota raised her hand. "I hate to break up this beautiful sisterly moment, but since we are in the honest bubble, I'm going to ask a question that is probably better left unasked."

She hesitated and took another long gulp from her champagne flute before continuing. "What about Gabe? Lotus, are you telling me that you felt nothing for him when you saw him? As much as you love Nick, no part of you wonders whether there is something that still needs to be resolved between the two of you, especially after everything that he said? I mean this was a man you were going to…"

"…end up heart-broken by," Lola interjected. "Let's not forget the London to Boston fiasco of 2005. He's no good. He shouldn't even be a topic of discussion."

Dakota shot her an irritated look from across the counter.

"For once, Lola, pa-leeze put your opinion on the backburner," she said as she turned back towards me.

Ignoring their argument, I lowered my head to counter to keep them from seeing my eyes. With my head still pressed between my arms, I could only whisper, "I can't stop thinking about him."

Their arguing stopped instantly.

I couldn't look at them as I continued to talk with my head buried.

"...I don't know what I am supposed to be feeling. Maybe, this is all hormonal. I *hope* that what I'm feeling is hormonal. I don't know if it's right or even fair, but I keep weighing the memories of things that I felt with him with the feelings that I have for Nick."

When I looked up at Lola, I was genuinely surprised to see a look of sympathy on her face.

"Lotus, you are not a horrible person. What you are feeling is normal. Every woman, everywhere, secretly has a shoulda-coulda-woulda or a Plan B guy. It's human nature, especially when things are challenging, to consider what you could have done in the past to change the present. Don't beat yourself up."

Feeling like I had already said too much, I wanted to shut up but I couldn't. This might be my only opportunity to tell anyone everything I felt, so I admitted one more thing.

"I also think about what would have happened had the nurse not come through the door when she did. If we had had another five minutes alone. I don't think I would have done anything, but I don't know, and that scares me. For a split second, I wanted him to kiss me. I wanted him to kiss me more than I wanted him not to kiss me. That scares the crap out of me, and that's why I want to go to Paris."

As soon as the words came out my mouth, I regretted saying them. Lola mumbled something under her breath as she shook her head, but Dakota was brave enough to say the obvious.

"Lotus, I understand why it seems like a good idea but you know you can't go to Paris so you can run away from Gabe. If you do, those feelings will obviously remain unresolved, and fester, waiting for the next time the universe forces you to cross each other's paths again."

TEN

I wonder if he would notice if I were choking, I thought as we sat across from each other in silence.

We had been eating Thai food at our kitchen counter for a half hour. It was hard to tell if Nick purposely hadn't looked at me or whether he was genuinely enthralled by the *New York Times* crossword puzzle he held in his hand since he arrived. His distracted mind usually wouldn't have bothered me, but now it felt like something more. The time that he normally needed to decompress after his classes now felt like full-blown avoidance.

I used to look forward to the quietness of our weekday evenings at home. Early in our relationship, because of the demands of our careers, I accepted that intimacy and chitchat were usually limited to the weekends. Now, the silence I had come to appreciate was a constant remainder of the unspoken discord between us. The pleasant kisses that we gave each other as we came and went felt more like those of roommates than of lovers; more like people living *around* each other than *with* each other.

When I looked up at him, the veins that pulsed from the sides of his temples confirmed that he was thinking about *something* other than his crossword puzzle and dinner. His constant reaching for his wine glass validated my suspicion. After another ten minutes had passed, I decided to bring up the elephant in the room.

"Are you sure there is no way for you to get out of the meeting tomorrow? I know it sounds silly, but I'm nervous about going to the first appointment by myself," I said, making an extra effort to not sound whiny.

He took a deep breath, finished his glass of wine, and put down his pen. "I'm sorry. I honestly feel terrible. If I could miss the presentation, I would, but the lecture will be focused on my research. Why are you nervous about going to the doctor?"

For the first time in a month, I felt like I had his full attention. I had spent most of the week preparing for my first doctor's appointment, writing down every question I could think to ask. I had a looming feeling that something was going to go wrong after browsing pregnancy websites for hours earlier that day.

"I know this is going to sound nuts, but what if I'm not pregnant? What if the test that I took in the ER was a false positive? Or what if I had an early miscarriage and didn't realize it?" I asked. "I haven't gained any weight. I haven't had any morning sickness. I'm eight weeks, and nothing has changed. I go to sleep a little earlier, but I could just be mildly depressed."

He didn't respond.

"I'm just scared," I finally admitted.

Nick's dark eyes looked tired as if I had already begun to exhaust him with my conversation. The expression on his face looked as if he regretted engaging me in the discussion.

"Lotus, you are neurotic. You and the baby are fine. Your appointment will just confirm what we already know. You are pregnant, and we are going to have a baby."

Obviously wanting to end the conversation, he stood from the table and walked into the living room. He stretched his long legs on the sofa and turned on the TV, which I knew was a clear signal that he wanted to be left alone. Though I was sure that it would annoy him, I followed him into the living room anyway, hoping that he would say something to comfort me.

"I'm serious. I've had no symptoms. I read a story about a woman who thought she was ten weeks pregnant, who had severe morning sickness and food aversions. But when she went for her first ultrasound there was nothing in her uterus..." I trailed off.

He stopped flipping through the channels and turned to face me as I sat on the chaise across the room. "That woman was an anomaly, Lotus, not the norm. I guarantee that you will not be a case study for any med school students or talked about on an unsolved medical mysteries show. Everything is fine. If you need me to, I'll cancel the lecture. I'll call my assistant tonight and have her send out a notice before the morning."

Despite his icy tone, this was his best attempt at being sympathetic. I felt foolish for telling him everything I had been thinking, but I couldn't dismiss the uneasy feeling that I had about tomorrow.

"Think about it like this," Nick added. "Either you are pregnant or you're not by way of some rare medical occurrence. If it turns out that you aren't pregnant, then fate would have dealt us a convenient hand. So in the bigger scheme of things, it's a win-win."

He stopped short of laughing when he saw the look on my face.

"Wait. That was a bad example, wasn't it?" he immediately asked.

"So if I'm not pregnant, that would be like winning the lottery for you, huh?" I asked as I had already begun to walk towards our bedroom.

Before I reached the hallway, he pulled me back into the room. As he towered over me, I looked for a glimpse of remorse in his eyes but I only saw embarrassment.

"That's not what I'm saying, Lo. I hope everything is okay, but if you aren't pregnant would that really be the worst thing in the world? Things would be back to normal, and there wouldn't be a need to put our life on hold. I'm just saying that wouldn't be a horrible thing. We could always have a baby later."

Because he didn't find anything wrong with what he was saying, I struggled to find the right words to say to him. I felt hurt, but equally and as strongly, I felt vindicated that my paranoia about his unhappiness was finally confirmed.

I pulled my arm from his grasp.

"I'm sorry that I derailed your life plans. Shit happens. You don't get the chance to shut me out or shut down. You don't get the chance to sulk for the next nine months because things haven't gone to your neatly mapped-out plan. I'm going to bed to rest. You can stay out here and figure out whether you can tolerate this detour that has occurred in our life."

That night we slept apart. The next morning when I woke up, he was already gone. On the nightstand next to our bed, I found a note.

Lo,

I'm sorry for last night. Have a great day today and call me when you leave the doctor. I love you and whatever it is growing inside of you, whether it's our son, daughter, a tapeworm, or an alien. Let's figure out our Plan B together.

I'm not going anywhere but where you are.

Nick

Even though he wasn't there, I knew that his words were genuine. I felt bad about some of the things that I had said to him the night before, but I was also relieved that we had finally talked about how he truly felt. It was nice to know that he wasn't planning to bolt out the door anytime soon, but I wanted to clear out the animosity that seemed to be growing between us.

I considered the prospect of moving to Paris. I imagined walking along the Seine and through the Latin Quarter, sharing croissants with a little girl. I imagined us walking through Notre-Dame and waiting in the long line outside the Louvre. I tried to imagine us picnicking on the wide lawn below the Eiffel Tower. I thought of her learning French as soon as she learned English, always having that extra perspective in her brain. Maybe she would grow up to be effortlessly chic? Even as I pictured how much fun Nick and I would have to drive her to see Versailles or taking her to see the Amalfi Coast, I still couldn't convince myself that it was something that *I wanted to do*. I loved Chicago. I liked the idea of having my family nearby when I had my first child. I wanted to talk to other moms who I wouldn't need a language dictionary to understand.

Still, Paris. I knew women who'd moved to much worse places for the sake of preserving a relationship. Just as I began to convince myself that something had to be wrong with me for not seeing this as the opportunity of a lifetime, my alarm clock went off and Michael Jackson's voice rang through my room, reminding me that I had less than an hour to get dressed and to my doctor's appointment.

***

When I walked into the women's wing of Lakeshore Memorial Hospital, I was greeted by a barrage of infographics pertaining to pregnancy. From conception to birth, various images of embryos, fetuses, and babies lined the walls of the main lobby and every woman there appeared to be pregnant or walking with a double stroller. Though I was reluctant to return to the hospital, the obstetrician referred to me by Lola practiced there, and supposedly the women's wing delivery suites were the poshest in the city. As I stood anxiously in the middle of the large atrium, which was filled with various reading rooms, gift shops and cafés, I felt like I was in the middle of a peaceful sanctuary. For the first time, I found myself feeling excited about the idea of being pregnant.

When I finally arrived at the reception desk to check in for my appointment, I was the only woman in the waiting room without a companion. I instantly wished that I had taken Lola up on her offer to come with me. While filling out the mounds of paperwork, I looked out the window across the span of buildings and bridges that connected the hospital's vast medical campus. When I spied the entrance to the emergency room a block and a half away, I quickly forced the thought of Gabe out of my mind. I had purposely parked as far away from the emergency room as possible just to ensure that there was no chance of running into him.

An hour later, after taking several vials of my blood, a nurse escorted me into a dark room where she told me to change into a pink gown and wait for my doctor. Once I was undressed, I sat on the examination bed and tried my best not to focus on the long white wand that was connected to the keyboard under the monitoring screen.

The vaginal probe had to be over eight inches long. Would it hurt? Just as I was bending to get a better look, the door opened and I saw a familiar round face smiling at me.

Dr. Solomon had been my sister's obstetrician through her two pregnancies, so I recognized her cherubim face, large bright brown eyes, and silver hair almost immediately. She was nearing retirement and not seeing any new patients, so Lola nearly had to beg her to see me as a new patient. Her smile immediately relaxed me, and despite all the possibilities running through my mind, it felt good to know that I was in good care.

After introducing herself to me formally, she told me to assume the position that I had come to dread since I was 18 years old: legs spread, knees up, and pelvis forward. As she positioned herself directly between my legs, I couldn't help but wonder whether she got annoyed looking at vaginas all day. Was it worse than my having to look at the executive director? I was trying to remember how many months had passed since my last bikini wax when I saw her reach for the magnum-sized wand. My body immediately tensed up.

"Too late to be nervous, my dear," the older Jewish woman said with a light laugh. "Soon enough, something much larger than this will be coming out of there."

Unsure of whether to be amused or put off by her candor, I laughed nervously. I relaxed all the muscles below my waist as she began to poke and prod, but the discomfort made it difficult. Closing my eyes, I decided to focus on the sound of the elevator music playing softly in the room as she continued to examine me, pushing buttons on the keyboard and pressing down on sides of my abdomen. After five minutes had passed in silence, thoughts of an empty uterus returned to my mind. Just when I opened my eyes to see if she looked worried, she pointed to the monitoring screen next to the bed. Suddenly, the sound of a rapid heartbeat filled the room.

When I looked at the monitor, I was surprised that I didn't see a picture of a round baby with recognizable features. Instead, there was just a small image of what appeared to be a teddy graham cracker, floating in a bubble.

Confused and worried I asked, "Is that it? Shouldn't it have feet, hands and legs?"

She smiled as if she was expecting the question.

"Don't be alarmed, dear. They are still forming and just too small to see at this point since the baby is the size of a walnut. By your next visit we will be able to see two arms and two legs, I promise."

I laid there in awe of the little creature on the screen, and my fears began to slip away. As the sound of its heartbeat continued to pulse through the speakers in the room, the gravity of my responsibility to it became clear. As unsure as I felt about whether Nick was ready to become a father, I was no longer afraid to become a mother. At that moment, being a mother was the only thing I felt fully capable of being.

It was too ridiculous to say aloud, but suddenly I could swear that I could feel the little image before my eyes within me. Without any further doubt, I embraced the baby's presence for the first time. I was overcome by the instant understanding that, as of that moment, its existence meant more to me than my own. Watching it drift slowly across the screen, I knew that I would do whatever was necessary to give him or her everything they would ever need.

Immediately, my brain began to generate a to-do list of things that needed to be done during the upcoming months. A registry of potential names began to file through my head. I started to wonder how much daycare would cost in France as opposed to Chicago. Quickly feeling inundated with details of what I thought was important, I looked back at the screen and the image of the small being inside of me reassured me that everything would work out the way that it is supposed to.

I left Dr. Solomon's office staring at the images from the ultrasound in my hand. I wished Nick had been able to hear the sound of our baby's heartbeat, but looking down at the picture it felt like he was there with me. Once I exited the elevator and stepped back into the atrium where I stood an hour before, I felt more certain than ever that everything would be okay.

Feeling happier than I had in weeks, I made a quick detour to a café in the lobby before heading to my car. I was determined to hold on to the joy that I felt no matter what, so I ordered hot chocolate with extra whipped cream from a freckle-faced teenage girl behind the counter. When she saw the picture in my hand, she smiled and said, "Here's to a perfect pregnancy." Though she had no idea that it had been anything but perfect so far, I smiled and thanked her, believing that her words were a good omen.

After she handed me my cup, I took a long sip and a feeling of complete peace washed over me. Still smiling, I bundled myself into my coat and scarf and prepared myself for the cold weather outside. Once I turned around, it took only one second before my body froze and the cup slipped from my hand.

He was on the other side of the large room, but our eyes immediately met as he took long strides towards me, in company with another doctor in scrubs. I turned to look for the nearest exit but realized it was too late to try to run. As he neared, our eyes never broke from each other. His expression revealed that he was as unenthused to see me, as I was to see him.

I tried to smile as I waited helplessly for them to reach me. Once they arrived at the counter, the freckled-face girl stood between the three of us as she vigorously cleaned up the hot chocolate I had spilled. Even as the other doctor continued to speak, Gabe's eyes didn't leave mine. When she finally paused to ask Gabe a question, he spoke to me.

"Are you here for a checkup?"

Noticing that the other doctor was now staring at us, I broke eye contact and looked down.

"Yes, I just had my eight-week checkup. Everything appears to be going well, so no worries here."

"Is your husband here?" Gabe cut me off though it was apparent that he knew the answer.

"Uh, no, I told him he didn't have to come since the hospital is just a few blocks away from my job," I lied, looking for an opportunity to excuse myself.

I had forgotten about the other doctor's presence until she extended her hand in front of me. As I reached forward to shake her hand, I immediately noticed the huge diamond on one of her fingers. When I finally looked at her, I was astonished to see how beautiful she was. At least six inches taller than I, she easily could have doubled as a model. Her thick, wavy hair was in a messy bun that just accentuated how perfect her bone structure was. Her bronzed skin was flawless; the only semblance of makeup was the subtle nude gloss glazed over her pouty lips. She was gorgeous in the way that I imagined made other woman hate her since the day she was born. But it was obvious from the way that she smiled at Gabe that she was in love with him.

She playfully nudged Gabe in the ribs. She smiled as she gave him a puzzled look.

"Since Gabe is being rude, I'll introduce myself. I'm Dr. Ashley McCann, Gabriel's fiancée. How do the two of you know each other?"

The 2ⁿᵈ Trimester

ELEVEN

"For the record, can I say that he is a major douche?" Lola whispered from the other end of the phone.

"…and not a flowery smelling Summer's Eve douche. He is like a cheap dollar store douche that leaves your vagina dry, itching and smelling like vinegar for a week after you use it."

Laughing, I peeked out my cracked door to make sure that I was still the only one in the office. I had to arrive at work in the wee hours of the morning to prepare for a board meeting to discuss our annual Venetian Night Gala, a fundraising event that drew some of the most prominent philanthropists, political figures and business people from across the city. Having attended the ball in the past, I initially jumped at the opportunity to sit on the planning committee since live jazz bands, silent auctions and champagne towers would normally epitomize a perfect night in my book. But after I began to suspect that the executive director planned to use it as an event to further his political fundraising needs, my interest in participating quickly diminished.

I had immersed myself in other projects and had scheduled as many meetings out of the office as I could to avoid working on the event. I thought I had eluded it all together until the week before when the executive director informed me that he wanted me to lead all of the planning efforts for the ball.

In previous years, the chair of the planning committee had always been one of our board members since they were some of the most influential business leaders in the city. Daily, I reminded myself that I couldn't screw up our most important event, even if I suspected that the executive director was trying to set me up for failure. Since law school, my career had been filled with contract negotiations, labor disputes, and white papers, so planning an event of this magnitude was something I had to figure out quickly.

Determined not to become a laughing stock, I had spent the last week becoming as proficient as possible in major donor fundraising and event planning. While still on the phone with Lola, I began to look over the stacks of documents I had prepared for the first meeting. From donor pyramids to vendor lists and a power point deck explaining customer relationship management products, I assured myself that I was prepared enough to get through it without looking incompetent.

"Hello...are you still there?" Lola whispered.

My thoughts were jolted back to why I called her. I shook my mouse to awaken my computer out of sleep mode. After scrolling through the hundreds of emails in my inbox, I found the one that I wanted to read to her.

"Sorry - I'm here," I replied once I opened the email with the subject line, **A Latte between Friends?**

"Lola, stop. He's not a douche for asking me to meet him for coffee. I'm the horrible person for allowing my mind to go *there*," I whispered as I began to separate copies of the work plan I had developed from the meeting agendas.

"It's a good thing that he is engaged, good for him. It's my fault for giving way too much energy to feelings that shouldn't even still be there. So it's no big deal. I may meet him. I may not. I'm not going to overthink it at this point. On another note, why are you still at home?"

"Because it's Good Friday, you heathen, and the kids are home from school. They are looking at a movie Mom got them about a turtle who died so all the other turtles could live. It's called, *Emmanuel, the Begotten Turtle Who Saved the World.*"

Like our mother, Lola somehow managed to balance being deeply cynical and fanatically religious, so it was difficult to tell if she was serious. To be on the safe side, I covered the mouth of the phone to muffle the sound of my laughter.

Hearing me, Lola whispered into the phone as she laughed, "That's why you are going to hell."

Once we both stopped laughing, I reluctantly asked her the same question I had when I first called her.

"Seriously, I need to prepare for this meeting. What do you think? Respond or just ignore it?"

"First things first, you recognize that the subject line is a double entendre, right?" she said as she began to eat something loud and crunchy that sounded like toast. "A **latte** between friends is the same as *A LOT* between friends. It's a loaded statement. It would be halfway cute if you weren't married and if he wasn't engaged and the former love of your life. But since you both are spoken for, that makes it inappropriate. My vote is to ignore it. Don't respond. He's baiting you for some reason and, Lotus, if you haven't figured it out yet, you have bigger things to worry about than flirting with an old boyfriend."

Other staff began to arrive in the office, and I could hear the phones beginning to ring on the other side of the door. Thinking about her last comment, I said, "Baiting me, for what? You are a bit paranoid. He's engaged, Lola."

"Don't be naïve, Lotus. Read it to me again," she demanded through the phone.

I looked down at the computer screen and read the words to myself before reading them aloud. I reminded myself of how much Lola hated Gabe and wished I had called Dakota instead. Clearing my throat, I read it to her.

Lotus,
> **I know you will be at the hospital a lot for your checkups so let's meet for coffee or lunch the next time you are here. A pregnant girl does have to eat, right?**
> > **Let me know,**
> > **Gabe**

It had been almost a month since I ran into him in the atrium of the women's wing, and I had done a good job of blocking him from my mind. Admittedly, I came home that day and searched the internet for his wedding website, a wedding announcement, and anything else that would provide information about his relationship with his Barbie-doctor-fiancée, but after a few hours I abandoned the mission filled with guilt-ridden shame. I accepted that Gabe had every right to be happy, and there was no reason to wish him anything less.

"Lotus, I make a living identifying dysfunction in the human brain. What I know for sure is this: A truly happy man – a man with no ulterior motive – does not reach out to an ex-girlfriend for coffee, lunch, or dinner. Especially after he just told you that he still thinks about what could have been. With your history, a happy man would barely want to acknowledge your presence. In fact, he would run as far away from you as possible."

I could hear my brother-in-law calling for her from somewhere in their house. As they exchanged loud yells about taking their dog to the groomer, I was a little relieved that she needed to get off the phone.

"Look, I'm sorry if I'm being judgmental, but you know how I feel about Gabe. He seems like the same self-centered bastard he was over ten years ago. *However*, I can hear Dakota in my head saying, 'Shut up, Lola' so here's what I think you should do. You are obviously curious, so have coffee with him. It is innocent, and it will be in a public place. Get it out of your system. Hopefully, by the end of it you will be able to close that chapter and move on."

I was about to remind her that I had moved on and that she had nothing to worry about when I was startled by the sound of someone knocking at my door.

"Sis, gotta go. For the record, I'm not curious; I just don't want to be rude. Goodbye," I whispered before gently laying the phone on its hook.

Looking down at the time on my computer I was stunned to see that an hour had passed and that the board meeting would be starting in less than fifteen minutes. I slid the various stacks of printouts on my desk into manila folders and yelled for the person to come in.

When the door opened, I was happily surprised to see the salty white hair on the woman facing away from me as she spoke to one of the office interns in the hallway. Elizabeth Harris, my mentor and the chair of the board of directors, stood there dressed in almost-uninterrupted black, the exception being the red soles of her stilettos that I spied while her back was to me. In her late sixties, she stylishly embodied sophistication and power. Despite her polished, upper-crust demeanor, she maintained a solid reputation for being fiercely intimidating and was secretly known as "The Ball Crusher" in certain social circles.

The heiress to a Manhattan real estate mogul, she had made a name for herself as a lobbyist in D.C over the course of forty years. After retiring from the firm that she started on K-Street, she moved to Chicago to teach, which was how I met her as a graduate student.

Over the past six years, as I oscillated through various jobs, she had persistently tried to get me to come to work for her foundation. I repeatedly turned down her informal job offers until one day I arrived at work to the news that the Governor, whom I worked for, was going to jail and that his Chief of Staff had been charged with crimes that ranged from misuse of campaign funds to soliciting underage women for sex. Afraid that I had unknowingly participated in some level of fraud, I called her that day from a bathroom stall and told her that I would take whatever job she was able to give me. One week later, I started at the Burnham Harris Foundation.

She stepped into my office and closed the door behind her. Her short, white, cropped haircut only highlighted her curt, no-nonsense demeanor. She smirked coyly before handing me a note as she looked at me through her chrome Gotti glasses.

"You look like crap, darling. Are you okay?" she said as she helped herself to the seat on the other side of my desk.

"I came bearing gifts. Would you like to know what your Jewish fairy godmother has done for you?"

I hadn't expected her to be at the meeting because I assumed she would be in New York for the Passover-Easter holiday weekend. Though she lived in Chicago, she maintained her family's estate in Westchester for the sole purpose of hosting her children and grandchildren on special occasions. The personal pictures that lined the walls of her Gold Coast office read like a United Colors of Benetton ad, with smiling faces on stylish people of almost every hue imaginable. Only those who knew her well were allowed to laugh when she divulged the nickname of her Westchester home, *The United Nations*, in private settings.

"I told your director that he needs to chair the gala his damn self this year. It's no secret that he will be using it for his fundraising purposes, so he needs to take the lead on this," she said, sounding mildly annoyed.

"Besides, the complexity of the civic and political community in this city can be a pain in the ass. But something told me that you wouldn't mind taking a back seat on this project."

The *complexity of the civic community in Chicago* had been a phrase that I had heard numerous times from her. She often joked that she moved here because it was the only other place in the country where "New York money could buy D.C-level access." Unlike so many other women who quickly develop a distaste for the boys-club mentality of the powerful social circle in Chicago, Elizabeth always found a way to thrive within it.

I walked around the desk and gave her a hug. I didn't have to explain to her why I was grateful. Still holding on to her hand I said, "Liz, you really are a life saver."

She placed her hand on my cheek, "Lotus, be prepared because you know he is going to be pissed. He will probably be a bit of an ass to you so, just for today, I need for you to be quiet, smile, and offer to take notes like a good girl, okay?"

I was slightly put off by her remark, but I made an extra effort to not look offended. Though I had come to know her better than most, there were elements of Elizabeth that I accepted that I may never understand, like why she continued to support the director when everyone at the Foundation knew that he was more interested in his political career than furthering the mission of the organization that she started. A part of me didn't want to know why she gave him such a long leash. She had shown herself to be a reliable and honest mentor and friend, so I decided that it was better to trust that she knew what she was doing than to ask too many questions.

Minutes later when we entered the same conference room where I almost had a nervous breakdown months before, I had the familiar feeling of being overwhelmed by testosterone. The oversized table in the small room with no windows resembled a gathering place for Mafioso or clergymen at a Papal Conclave. Though we entered the room together, Elizabeth and I went in two different directions. She confidently walked to the head of the table while I tried to remain invisible as I slid into a seat against the back wall.

Next to her sat the executive director, who had been glaring at me from the moment that I walked into the room. Elizabeth greeted everyone before asking him to close the door; her usual signal to everyone that she was ready to begin the meeting. To everyone's surprise but mine he snapped back at her, "That's what I pay my managing director to do."

Loud enough for everyone in the room to hear, Elizabeth leaned towards him and whispered, "I can make your fundraising very easy or very difficult for you, sir. Your choice."

The discomfort throughout the room was palpable. Embarrassed, the executive director stood from his chair without saying anything and shut the conference room door before returning to his seat to sulk.

"Gentlemen, I apologize for cutting into the beginning of your holidays, but it's the end of March, and we must begin to think about our annual gala. But first, I brought some delicious flourless chocolate cake from my favorite kosher bakery in Lincoln Park to make this meeting a little less painful."

Motioning towards the cake box and plates in the middle of the table, she encouraged us to eat. "Please enjoy. I insist."

Though the men on the board of directors included some of the most powerful businessmen in the city, everyone in the room seemed afraid to move. After a minute passed, and no one stirred, I got up and cut myself a large piece since I was very hungry. When I returned to my seat, I looked up and saw Elizabeth peering towards me with a satisfied smile.

"Since Lotus is the only one here with an appetite, I'll presume that's my cue that I can start the meeting," she said, writing something on the white board behind her.

"I promise to keep things short. In a nutshell, we need to double our fundraising goal from last year. So, gentlemen, get ready to shake some trees and flex your muscles because our goal for this year is one million dollars." She stepped away from the board that now displayed the number in bold handwriting.

The goal seemed to stun everyone in the room except the executive director, which no one seemed to notice but me. All of the men surrounding the table began to reposition themselves awkwardly in their chairs. The goal was audacious to say the least, and it likely meant that most of those present would have to contribute personally.

No one spoke as Elizabeth continued to communicate her vision for the gala. When the meeting was over, the room cleared quickly as the men wasted no time in making their way back to their homes and offices before the holiday weekend officially began.

As I sat in the back of the room gathering my things, I wondered about Elizabeth's true motive for removing me as the chair of the planning committee. Assuming that she had already left to catch her flight to New York, I was startled when she suddenly appeared in the doorway of the room.

"Come to the table. Let's talk over another piece of cake, shall we?" she suggested.

After gathering my folders, I moved into the seat next to her. Without asking, she cut me a large piece of cake and handed it to me with a smile.

"You know dear, people call me a philanthropist because of my financial contributions to things that I am passionate about, like education and poverty. Some call me a humanitarian because of the hundreds of buildings and programs that have my family's name attached to them," she said as she made her cake disappear in small, lady-like bites.

"But the truth is that I like to think of myself as an investor. That mindset is how I became successful as a lobbyist. A successful career at anything is contingent on the success of the relationships that you build. The success of your relationships that you build is contingent on the investments that you are willing to make." She paused before continuing.

"I tell you all of that to say that our relationship is strong because not only do I consider you to be a wonderful mentee but I also consider you to be a great investment. Do you understand?"

Unsure why I was beginning to feel uneasy, I took another bite before responding to her. The cake was delicious, no surprise, because Elizabeth had great taste in everything.

"Of course, Elizabeth. I appreciate everything that you have done for me personally and professionally."

"I know you were reluctant to come and work here initially because of our relationship, but when the opportunity presented itself, I immediately brought you on to the team, didn't I?

I did that because I see you as an asset, do you understand?"

She didn't do it often, but from time to time Liz would remind me that I was professionally beholden to her. I would never say it to her, but her unknown expectations often felt like a sword hanging over my head. I was now obligated to stay aligned with her interests, and this often added a layer of stress I wish that I didn't have to consider.

"Yes, Liz. I understand."

I felt her eyes on me even without looking from the slice of cake in front of me. Though I wanted to ignore her stare, I couldn't disregard the sudden tension in the room.

When I finally looked up at her, her typically warm brown eyes appeared sharp and focused.

"When the director wins his Senate race, who do you think is going to take his place?"

It was the first time I had considered the possibility.

"Honestly, I hadn't thought much about it. To be completely frank, I never considered that he would win the race."

She gave a patronizing sigh. "Lotus, I've known for more than two years that he was going to run for office. I wouldn't allow him to use my gala as his private piggy bank if he weren't going to win. But more than that, I'm a bit surprised that you didn't consider that I created this position for you so you would be able to one day take his place," she said, sounding more upset than I had ever heard.

It was the opportunity I had been waiting for my entire career, but the prospect of her offer only made me feel apprehensive. I was confident that I could lead the foundation, but nothing within me wanted to base my entire career off of quid pro quos, which was an understood expectation of the position. As much as I loathed the executive director, he was more apt for a lifetime of board meetings and donor lunches than I ever imagined myself becoming.

I searched for the right words to say in response, but she stopped me.

"But more than that, Lotus, for the past two hours all I've been trying to figure out is when you were going to have enough respect for me as your mentor and as the person who gave you this opportunity to tell me that you are pregnant."

TWELVE

"I know you were faking it, but I'll take it," Nick said as he kissed me and headed for the shower.

Lying in the bed, I continued to pant loudly until he was out of sight on the other side of the bathroom door. Enjoyable sex felt like a distant memory, especially since my tiny baby bump had begun to make its discreet debut. The feeling of my small belly rubbing up against his torso was something — along with the constant soreness of my growing bustline — that I hadn't become accustomed to.

I was feeling constantly bloated, slightly unattractive, and perpetually stressed. Sex had been the furthest thing from my mind for months. It may have been the guilt that I felt for not fulfilling some unspoken wifely duty or guilt over the fact that I hadn't told him about my plans to meet Gabe later that day, but I woke up determined to break our dry spell. I thought my performance was worthy of an Academy Award, but Nick obviously knew me better than I realized.

When I saw him step into the shower, I peeked at the alarm clock beside the bed. I still had a few hours until I had to be at the hospital, but I wished that the day were already over.

"Have you spoken to Liz yet?" he yelled from the shower.

"No," I said, reminded of the strife that still lingered between her and me.

Almost four weeks had passed since our last meeting where I had tried to convince her that I wasn't purposely hiding my pregnancy. Though she didn't say it outright, it was apparent that she felt betrayed. Every week that followed, I had attempted to meet her for lunch or coffee to explain everything — why I hadn't told her sooner and that there was a possibility that Nick and I would be moving by the end of the summer — but had no luck.

"Why don't you just email her?" Nick asked.

"Because I feel like I owe it to her to explain everything face to face," I explained.

"Well, it's not like she can fire you," he said as he rinsed his hair under the stream of hot water. "Even if she is pissed off, your job is protected, at least until the baby comes. After that, you probably won't have to worry about working there anyway, right?"

I took a deep breath before walking into the bathroom to brush my teeth. Nick was many things, but subtle wasn't one of them. Since Easter, he mentioned Paris increasingly, reminding me of our agreement to make a decision by the end of May. Though he said the deferment was still on the table, it felt like his mind was already made up. His assurances that he would stay if that's what we agreed to be best for our family felt less and less convincing. It felt like no matter what, our decision would be based on what he wanted. As much as I tried to fight it, it was difficult to not resent him especially since my fear was that he was inherently unable to put anyone – including our child – above his ambitions.

"Way to be pragmatic, but it's about more than my job, Nick. I respect Liz, and I don't want her to be upset with me. I feel like she has taken the news of this pregnancy personally, like it was an affront to her in some way. It just doesn't make any sense to me."

As he stepped out of the shower and began to dry off, I saw the wary look on his face.

"What are you thinking?"

His expression turned sympathetic. I expected him to tell me that I should quit my job and become a barista at Starbucks since we would be moving away anyway.

"I know you respect Liz and I'm sure that she cares for you personally. I just don't think you should be naïve when it comes to her. She's smart, and she told you that she became successful by learning how to manipulate people to get what she wants. At this point, your only worry should be our family. Elizabeth will be just fine."

Surprised that he didn't minimize the entire situation, I was appreciative that he didn't see it as an opportunity to insert Paris into our conversation. The suggestion that Liz might be manipulating me was something that I wasn't willing to consider.

Seeing my discomfort, he changed the subject. "Are you sure you are okay going to the doctor by yourself?" he asked as he slipped on his khakis and reached for his purple polo shirt hanging on the back of the bathroom door.

"Sure. I'll be fine. Just don't forget about the appointment in four weeks. I want you to be there because that's when we will find out the baby's gender," I reminded him.

"I won't forget. I promise. Don't worry about Elizabeth. She'll eventually come around," he said before he grabbed his bag, kissed me, and headed to work.

***

After my appointment with Dr. Solomon, I made a quick stop in the restroom to check my appearance. My hair, which had begun to grow like a tumbleweed, made a halo of wild curly strands around my head. Looking at myself under the bright halogen lights, I thought about how different I looked from the girl Gabe knew in college. My eyes looked tired. I no longer tried to hide the freckles that surrounded my nose with makeup. My previously athletic build had grown curvier and softer.

As I critically dissected parts of myself that I hadn't noticed the day before, I became irritated with myself for having agreed to meet him. Hoping that it wasn't too late to back out, I checked my watch and realized that we were scheduled in the atrium in less than five minutes. Rolling my eyes at myself through the mirror, I applied the only lip-gloss that I remembered to throw in my purse that morning and prayed that our coffee date would be brief.

This is destined to be the most uncomfortable cup of coffee I will ever drink; I thought after deciding to mention his fiancée up front. I convinced myself that there would be no reason to feel guilty about seeing him if we focused on our significant others; it would simply be two friends catching up on each other's lives. My conscience would be clear.

When I exited the elevator, I saw Gabe standing near the coffee stand where we had bumped into each other a few weeks earlier. Even from across the room, the seriousness of his expression was intimidating. Neither of us moved towards each other, so I wasn't sure if he spotted me. It wasn't until I saw a cautious smile spread across his lips that I realized that he saw me. As he waved to me, his expression softened, and his eyes immediately appeared sweet and kind. Before I could begin to move in his direction, he began to walk towards me.

"Hi," he said as he leaned in and gave me an awkward hug. When my belly brushed against his, I instantly felt uncomfortable and pulled away. Hoping that he didn't notice, I pointed behind him to the coffee stand.

"Hey, Doctor, I could have met you over there. Or are you trying to get out of paying already?" I joked.

He hesitated for a millisecond trying to see if I was serious. When he realized I was joking, he smiled.

"My shift just ended and I'm off for the day. Coffee will keep me up through the night at this point so do you want to have lunch instead?" he asked.

It must have been obvious that I was trying to think of an excuse. Before I could come up with anything that was remotely believable, he looked like he was prepared to force the issue.

"I've never met a pregnant woman who didn't want to eat. I promise I won't keep you too long," he said with his arm in the pledge position.

The truth was that I was starving since I hadn't eaten breakfast, but I was unconvinced that having a meal with him was a good idea. I reached to find my phone in my purse, hoping that miraculously someone would call me so I could have an excuse to leave.

"You're ridiculous," he said.

Before I could object, he grabbed my hand and guided me towards the escalators on the other side of the room.

"The cafeteria upstairs is one of the best on campus. I promise that you will not regret this."

I could feel the sweat forming on my forehead and palms as we walked across the room together. Once we got to the escalator, I expected him to release my hand but he continued to hold on to it. Despite my nervousness, I didn't pull away until we arrived at the landing of the next floor.

"Okay, Gabe, you've successfully kidnaped me. I promise I won't bolt for the door," I said as I jammed both hands into my dress pockets.

"Good. You of all people should know that I don't bite," he said as we walked down the long hallway towards what appeared to be a large dining room.

To my surprise, the hospital's cafeteria was an expansive food court that spanned across most of the second floor. It housed a seemingly endless number of food stations offering cuisines from around the world. After spending several minutes overwhelmed by all of the choices, I decided on a falafel sandwich, home fries and two sushi rolls to go. Once I made my way to the pay station, I was told that my meal was already paid for, and directed to the dining area where I could see Gabe sitting in the furthest corner of the room.

When I finally arrived at the table, he looked at my plate and laughed.

"What?" I asked feeling a little embarrassed.

"I'm laughing at all the food on your plate," he admitted as he bit into his hamburger. "And don't blame it on the baby because you have always been greedy."

I smiled but purposely shifted my eyes away from him. Since the day I arrived in the emergency room I couldn't help but notice how much he hadn't changed. His gray eyes were still sincere but melancholy. His smile was still modest. Obviously, he still laughed whenever he was nervous.

Within minutes, the apprehension I had felt was almost completely gone. When he spoke, he still had a way of making me feel like I was the only one in the room. His eyes remained fixed on me, even as I nervously stuffed my food in my mouth. Unexpectedly, his tales from the ER made me laugh so hard that the sides of my stomach began to hurt. Laughing uncontrollably at one of his stories, I could see from the smile on his face that he was enjoying our time as much as I.

I had forgotten how easy it had always been to talk to him and deep down wished that somehow we could become friends. We went on to debate everything from the merits of universal healthcare to who was likely to win the NBA finals. He proudly showed me the tribal tattoos he had received on his forearms while volunteering in Kenya with Doctors Without Borders.

Listening to him talk about everything he had accomplished, it was bittersweet to realize that he had achieved so much of what he dreamed about when we first met. I had always felt that we were both too young to know what we wanted, or where our lives could take us, but listening to him, I realized that he always knew exactly where his life would take him. Despite everything that had happened between us, I envied him because he had never been afraid to go after what he wanted.

He stopped talking mid-sentence. "I'm talking too much about myself. I think I'm afraid that if I stop talking, you will get up and leave. So come on, it's your turn. Tell me about your life and how you are doing. Most important, how is your pregnancy going?"

I was caught completely off guard by his question. For some reason, I had assumed that my pregnancy, just like the things he said to me in the emergency room, would be off limits for discussion.

"I feel fat," I blurted out, wanting to keep our conversation as lighthearted as possible. "I also keep having weird pains in my vagina, and I know this is too much information, but I keep having gas - horrible, loud and obnoxious gas. I'm also certain that my breasts weigh about 15 pounds each. But, other than those small few issues, I'm doing great."

He laughed so loudly that people sitting on the other side of the dining room turned in our direction. When he wiped tears from the corner of his right eye, I remembered how easily he cried when he thought something was truly funny. I didn't know why his laughter made me so happy, but it did. When I felt myself staring at him for too long, I forced myself to look away.

"You look beautiful and I sincerely mean that. The bones in your pelvis are beginning to move around to accommodate the baby. That's why you are having pains in your...vagina. The gas is normal and your 15-pound breasts, though hilarious to imagine, are also normal," he said as he wiped his eyes one last time.

Between mentions of my vagina and breasts, I knew that I was enjoying my time with him more than I should. Returning my attention back to my plate I reached for a piece of sushi with my chopsticks. In a flash, Gabe snatched it from my grasp and put it on his plate.

"If you wanted some sushi, I could have gotten you an extra roll," I joked.

"No, I hate sushi," he said, pushing his plate to the side. "But you shouldn't eat it either."

His face was surprisingly serious and instinctively I knew it wasn't about the sushi. There was something that he wanted to say, but he appeared as leery as I was of deviating from our light mood. Neither of us said anything until I finally asked him the one question that I had been wondering since I received his initial invitation.

"Why did you want to meet?"

"Because I wanted to apologize," he immediately responded.

"Uh, for what?" I asked condescendingly, surprised that I couldn't do a better job hiding the sarcasm in my voice.

"For what I said to you that day in the emergency room. I recognize that it was selfish and inappropriate. I was more concerned about getting some things off my chest than about your feelings. I would have never said any of that to you if I knew you were about to find out that you were pregnant."

"So the fact that I'm married *and* the fact that you are engaged wasn't enough of a reason, Gabe?" I asked, thinking of the litany of horrible things Lola had always said about him.

"No, it wasn't," he answered with surprising indifference.

"No?" I repeated, unsure of whether I heard his response correctly.

"I said no, Lotus. Your marriage and my engagement were obviously not enough to keep me from telling you how I felt."

In my shock, it was difficult to know whether his candor should be attributed to his integrity or his arrogance.

"Wow. You ARE an asshole," I said under my breath.

"Look, I accepted the way that I feel about you a long time ago. I'm okay with those feelings regardless of how inconvenient, ill-timed, and unrealized they have to remain. When I saw you, the only thing that mattered was telling you what I needed to say. That need trumped the fact that I can't do anything about how I've always felt about you. So, no, I wasn't thinking about your husband or my fiancée. My only goal was not to miss an opportunity to tell a woman whom I will always love that I'm sorry for hurting her."

"On that note, have a good day," I said as I quickly began to stack my plates onto my tray.

"Lotus, I'm sorry," he said as he held onto my tray, keeping me from picking it up.

"Are you in love with her?" I inadvertently shouted though I knew I had no right to. I didn't even know if I wanted to hear his answer.

I hoped that he would say yes because that would give me a reason never to speak to him again. I wanted to be able to leave him sitting in the back of the cafeteria knowing without a doubt that he was a horrible person. I needed a reason to leave everything good that I ever thought about him there at the table.

"It's complicated," he responded.

"What does that mean?" I asked, unwilling to accept such a generic answer.

"Do I love Ashley? Yes, I do," he said quietly with a sense of resignation in his voice. "We met two years ago after I was promoted to attending physician. We dated for almost a year, and she became pregnant. I didn't know if I was ready to marry her, but I proposed because I thought about how I felt when my parents separated, and I didn't want that for my child."

He looked around the cafeteria. I suspected that he was looking to make sure that Ashley wasn't in the room until I saw tears developing in his eyes.

"She miscarried at the end of her second trimester and I couldn't bring myself to call things off. I knew that I didn't want to spend the rest of my life with her, but I owed her too much to leave her at that painful moment. We needed each other during that time. So, yes, I love Ashley but I'm not in love with her. I was willing to spend the rest of my life with her even though I've always known that she wasn't the person who I want to be with."

THIRTEEN

We all have moments that play out in our minds long before we know if they will ever happen.

How to react to a surprise party for you. How to respond to a proposal you are anticipating. How to cry, but still appear photogenic at one's wedding.

We all dream that these moments, if they ever come true, will celebrate us, vindicate us, and prove our worth.

Of all the moments-to-come that I'd imagined, the one I'd thought about most would occur on a warm summer day. My hair would look perfect, and my makeup would be flawless. The dress that I had on would accent my perfectly toned Pilates and Yoga-sculpted body. The glimmer from the five-carat diamond on my left hand would blind people who were walking towards me on the street.

I imagined that I would see Gabe from a distance and our eyes would meet. We would both smile, silently acknowledging each other as our paths slowly intersected. Once we met in the middle of the sidewalk, he would immediately apologize for everything that he had done; I would tell him that I hadn't thought about 'all that stuff' in years. I would tell him that I forgave him and kiss him one last time on the cheek. When he asked if I wanted to catch up over drinks I would tell him that I couldn't because my husband and I had to hop our private jet to Mau'i.

Contrary to how I imagined I would feel, as I sat listening to everything I had waited a decade to hear, the only thing I felt was an overwhelming sense of sadness and anger. I tried to convince myself that I now had permission to hate him but knew that would never happen. I wanted to leave, but my legs felt cemented to the ground. I sat there, listless, weighing my need to tell him how much he had hurt me in the past with the fact that I knew that I should no longer care.

"Did you ever think about me?" he asked out of nowhere.

I pulled money out of my purse and laid it on the table.

"Thank you for lunch, Gabe. Here's some money to cover the cost of my food," I said, grabbing my coat and purse. He tried to grab my hand again, but I quickly pulled it away.

"I'm sorry about what happened to you and Ashley. But that doesn't give you the right to ignore my marriage because you see our interactions as opportunities to get things off your chest. It's selfish, and if you loved me half as much as you believe you do then you would know that. Grow up and leave me alone."

"Do you really want me to do that?" he asked.

"What do you want me to say? Yes, I want you to leave me alone. Once upon a time I loved you and would have done anything to be with you. Now, I've chosen my husband and you need to choose your fiancée. I've moved on with my life. I suggest that you do the same."

I walked away as fast as I could to the point that I was almost running. As I moved through the hallway past the row of rooms that led to the escalator, I cursed myself for not listening to Lola. A stream of tears ran down my face until the neckline of my dress was completely wet against my body.

By the time I neared the end of the corridor, I was trembling and pulled my phone out of my purse to call Lola. Before I had an opportunity to press the first number, I felt his hand on my arm pulling me backward until I found myself in an empty meeting room.

I didn't have time to yell.

With my arms pinned against the door, I tried to break away from his grip. Within seconds, his hands cusped the back of my head as he lowered his face to mine.

I couldn't stop crying, but I also couldn't resist him.

He kissed the side of my mouth, my cheeks and down my neck until settling firmly on my lips. Each kiss was followed by waves of both guilty pleasure and paralyzing fear. As he gripped my hair, his kisses were deliberate and passionate. Even with my eyes closed, I knew that the tears on my face weren't mine alone. Instead of opening my eyes to face the mistake I was making, I allowed myself to revel in the taste of his lips. I hadn't forgotten them, but I hadn't remembered them being this sweet, either.

A voice inside of me screamed to leave, but a small corner of my heart kept me from moving. My clenched fists wanted to hit him, but instead they remained powerless by my sides.

His hands moved from my face until they clutched my lower back. It took a moment to realize that I was holding him as tightly as he was holding me. It wasn't until my phone rang that my mind was forced to recognize the gravity of what we had just done.

Unable to speak, I stepped away from him in a state of disbelief.

"I'm sorry," he whispered as he stood inches away from me still holding my hand.

"No, you're not," I said before wiping the tears off my face and walking out the door.

FOURTEEN

Their faces confirmed the guilt that I had felt for the past twenty-four hours. One bottle of wine in, they continued to sit at the table in silence. I urged them to speak - to say anything - but it was apparent that they didn't know how to respond.

From across the table, Dakota forced a kind smile in an attempt to let me know that she wasn't judging me. I had already recounted the story to them twice, telling them every detail of the events of the previous morning. Even as I recalled the story aloud, I tried to find the exact moment that I suspended all logic and nearly destroyed my marriage. With each second that passed without them saying anything, I feared they would never look at me the same way.

The restaurant where we chose to meet was oddly appropriate for the occasion. The steakhouse, which was nested on the bottom floor of the Chicago landmark hotel, was known to have been a secret brokering place for politicians, businessmen, and even the mob. The aged cherry oak that furnished the walls and low-hanging lights seemed to provide the perfect ambiance for disclosing a shameful secret. The heavy remnants of cigar smoke would have otherwise made me nauseous if I hadn't been too distracted in my thoughts to notice.

Annoyed, our waiter arrived back at the table after we had sent him away twice. As he approached us for a third time, Dakota spoke up.

"We are going to need another bottle of your house Cabernet," she said with a smile that was both polite and mildly dismissive.

Restraining his obvious irritation that we hadn't ordered any food yet, he smiled with equal condescension.

"Fine choice, ladies, I'll bring out another basket of dinner rolls as well."

Once he disappeared behind the restaurant kitchen's large wooden doors, I finally asked, "Have I completely ruined my marriage and should I tell Nick what I've done?"

"No," they both said.

"No," Lola repeated.

"Nope. No. No. No. No. No." Dakota echoed passionately as if what I had suggested was more egregious than the act itself.

Lola nodded in agreement. "Lo, many marriages have survived far worse, believe me. You need to take this to the grave with you."

I wanted - and needed - for them to tell me exactly what I should do. I hadn't slept all night and every time Nick said anything to me I wanted to cry. I had spent an hour that morning scrubbing my skin and brushing my teeth, trying somehow to erase the guilt. Now that I should be on my way home, I wanted to avoid going back there as long as possible.

Lola broke the silence. "Just for the record, can I say that I really, really HATE Gabe? I mean, I really hate him. Before, I thought I did, but I just realized that there is a completely new level of hate that I never realized exists. It's like, I know I shouldn't say this, but I secretly hope this all ends in his untimely and unfortunate demise."

I was grateful for the laugh though Dakota seemed slightly irritated by the comment. It was comforting to know that I could feel something other than guilt. As I continued to laugh uncontrollably, I saw Lola and Dakota's worried stares from across the table until I suddenly broke down into a torrent of tears.

"I don't think I will be able to keep this from Nick. I made a mistake but isn't keeping it from him more of a betrayal?" I asked them just as the waiter returned with a second bottle of wine.

"Say nothing," Lola said as she handed me her napkin to dry my face.

"Telling him would be for you, not him. Right now, you can say it was just a kiss but for Nick it would mean much more. You would hurt him badly for no good reason, and you would run the risk of his ego never being able to forgive you. Forgive yourself for making a mistake and move on. Do not say anything." She motioned her hands over her mouth to simulate zipping my lips.

She was right, but the idea that time might somehow erase the memory of what I did seemed implausible. Though Nick hadn't been at home much in the past day, the few times that we spoke, I couldn't allow myself to look him in the eye. Even as he tried to kiss me on his way to work, I shifted my mouth out of his way. Luckily, he was too preoccupied with his phone to notice; he planted a quick kiss on my cheek before heading out the door.

"Lotus, do you want to stay in your marriage?" Dakota asked out of nowhere.

"You can erase the memory of what happened yesterday out of your mind. Trust me; I know that it can be done. If you want to forget about what happened, then none of us have to ever speak of it again. However, I'm not sure if you want to forget what happened. So you need to either let Gabe go for good or make some very hard decisions about your marriage before you do something that you won't be able to forgive yourself for."

The typical bluntness of her advice felt exceptionally cold, but it was what I needed to hear. I had never admitted aloud exactly what she seemed to suspect; for almost five months, since the day I first ran into Gabe in the emergency room I began to imagine what life might be like if we had stayed together.

"This is completely f-ed up," I said to no one in particular.

"Yep, that's about right," Lola said while finishing off another glass of wine.

From a distance, I could see our waiter heading towards us.

Dakota noticed him too and said, "Come on. We need to order something before he finds a reason to kick us out."

We all began to look quickly through our menus for the first time, trying to find something that we could split. When he finally arrived at the table, Lola began to order.

"I know you hate us, sir, but I promise that we are great tippers. So bring us another Shirley Temple for her, some stuffed mushrooms, chicken wings and bruschetta for the table, and I promise that we will compensate you for your time."

For the first time since we arrived, he smiled genuinely before turning to leave. Lola waited until he was out of earshot before her voice became cryptic.

"We can try to convince you not to see him again. We can try to show you all the ways that you are very close to screwing up your marriage. If you have already made up your mind that you aren't ready to leave Gabe the hell alone, then you will find a way to see him. You will find a way to bump into him or maintain some level of contact until exactly what you say you don't want to happen does happen, and you are forced to make a decision that should be made right now - before things go any further."

FIFTEEN

Don't screw up your marriage.

For weeks, Lola's warning echoed through my mind as soon as I woke up.

During the month that followed I did nothing but focus on the gala and try to convince myself that I would be happy living in Paris. Nick's aloofness continued without any clear explanation, and I couldn't help but wonder if he would become even more distant once the baby arrived. As much as moving to Paris would have excited me a year ago, the real possibility of raising a child there virtually alone was petrifying. Yet, as the deadline for making a final decision grew closer, I told myself that if moving was what I needed to do to save my marriage and keep my family together then it was the only decision I could make.

I buried the kiss with Gabe so far in the back of my mind that it became easier and easier to believe that it never happened.

In the context of the sixty- or seventy-year marriage Nick and I would enjoy together, it wouldn't mean anything. It would be a small blemish on a lifetime of being honest and committed to my husband. Not that I could imagine what it would feel like to be married sixty years, but I had every intention of taking my secret to the grave.

Memorial Day came quickly and I prepared myself for the various events that lay ahead for Nick and me that holiday weekend: finding out the gender of the baby, making a decision on Paris and celebrating my 31st birthday. To mark the occasions, Nick planned for us to spend the long weekend together at a bed and breakfast in Lake Geneva - a small, quaint resort town - which was two hours north of the city.

Early Friday morning Nick and I woke up early to finish packing. Though we had promised to make the trip strictly for rest and relaxation, I wasn't surprised to see him packing his briefcase, papers, and laptop.

Clenching my teeth, I forced myself not to complain because I didn't want our weekend to get off to a bad start. My slight annoyance must have been obvious because when he caught me staring at him, he looked remorseful.

"You go to sleep at 7:00 o'clock. What else am I supposed to do for four days?" he asked.

An hour later, we stood together at our front door looking at a row of ten bags in front of us.

"Ten bags for 96 hours?" he asked.

"If this is what it takes to go to Wisconsin for the weekend, can you imagine how many boxes we are going to need when it's time to move?"

His presumptuousness surprised me. I didn't know if he was referring to our potential move to Paris or a day in the distant future when we would move to another home. Believing that he was a bit audacious, I forced myself to remember that it didn't matter. As he picked up the first in the series of bags, I dismissed my thoughts and handed him his car keys.

I went through our house a final time to make sure that we had everything that we needed. After double-checking to make sure that we didn't leave our toothbrushes, I felt my phone vibrate in my coat. Assuming it was one of my parents or Lola sending me early birthday wishes, I reached into my pocket to grab it. Before I could finish reading the short message, a knot developed in my throat.

Happy Birthday, My Puna.

Gabe

My Puna.
Punarbhava.
I sat on the edge of the bed reading the words over and over again. My mind took me to the day Gabe and I first met, when I walked into my calculus professor's office only to find Gabe helping the students who signed up for tutoring. As he sat behind the large oak desk in the musty-smelling old room, I was intimidated by both his looks and intellect. Over the course of

an hour, instead of paying attention to his tips on understanding chain theory, I followed every movement of his lips. Unable to retain any information from the session, I asked him if I could come back the following week. After checking his calendar he agreed, just before inquiring about my name.

"Lotus...that's a unique name. Your parents must wear tie-dye shirts and smoke a lot of weed, huh?" he asked as he began to pack his book bag.

I had grown accustomed to people making fun of my name so I prepared myself for the litany of jokes I assumed would follow. Long resolved to not take jests about my name personally, I responded with an exaggerated chuckle before giving him a blank and annoyed stare.

"No, not exactly," I said as I began to gather my things as quickly as possible. "It has nothing to do with weed, LSD or Charles Manson if that was what you were about to say next."

After I had shoved the last of my books into my backpack, I looked up to see him staring peculiarly back at me. His eyes searched mine for something, as if he was waiting for me to unveil a big secret. After a few seconds of feeling uncomfortable, I blurted out, "What?"

"Punarbhava, right?"

Punarbhava.

Other than my family, I hadn't met anyone who knew the word, let alone someone who pronounced it correctly. Outside of Tibetan Monks and Yogis, few people knew that my name referred to the Buddhist concept of Punarbhava, a Sanskrit word that meant rebirth and to experience a spiritual reawakening. My mother, a religion major in college, chose it because of the long series of miscarriages she had between Lola and me. She said that my birth felt like God had allowed her a *new beginning*, a *second chance to be what made her the happiest – a mother.*

I explained to Gabe that for that reason, even as an adult, she still referred to me as *"My Puna."*

Heart racing, I looked down at the phone and immediately deleted the message. When I heard the door opening again, I shoved my phone back into my coat pocket and thoughts of Gabe far out of my mind.

***

We entered the waiting area of Dr. Solomon's suite and found seats between two giddy and happy-looking couples. As we sat there together, Nick appeared distracted and uncomfortable, far beyond his normal preoccupation with his thoughts. I nudged him and asked if everything was okay after watching him stare vacantly at his tablet for several minutes.

"Sorry, I just have a lot of work emails coming through this morning," he said without looking up at me.

I hid my disappointment that he didn't appear to be the least bit excited about the appointment. Looking at the visible intimacy of the other couples surrounding us, I wondered what was wrong with us, why we didn't seem to share their same excitement. Hurt at how disinterested he appeared, I was relieved when a nurse called my name and directed us to an ultrasound examination room just behind the doors.

I positioned my feet in the stirrups in front of the bed after getting undressed. Seeing Nick sitting with a clear view of my birth canal, I tried to lighten the mood.

"Will you be able to handle seeing something the size of a watermelon coming out of there?" I asked, gesturing beneath my gown.

Without laughing, he looked up from his phone and said, "We have a lot to talk about this weekend, right?"

I wondered if he was purposely trying to spoil the moment for both of us. After five and a half months of making excuses for his detachment, I found his lack of self-awareness infuriating and disturbing. Ignoring him, I closed my eyes and anticipated seeing our baby. Though still somewhat of an apparition, in moments like this, he or she was a needed reminder of the love that we shared.

A gust of air from the vent behind Nick blew directly between my legs. Feeling my body immediately tense up, I tried my best to relax. There was a growing anxiety between us that made him feel farther away than usual. I wished that I knew the right thing to say to him as much as I needed him to say the right thing to me. I could tell him that I was willing to choose us over what I wanted, but I needed him to assure me that he was willing to do the same.

As he sat across the room more attentive to his phone than to me, I missed the friend in him that I had grown to love, the friend who always found a way to assure me that everything would be okay. He now felt like a bad imitation of the man I'd known, but I had no explanation as to why, only a suspicion.

We both jumped when we heard knocking at the door. Dr. Solomon appeared seconds later, smiling cheerfully.

"So I finally get to meet the baby's father, eh? I started to believe that she made you up, Dad! You must be very excited about today," she said, giving me a wink as she walked over and typed on the keyboard under the monitor.

She applied drops of clear crème on my round belly and began navigating the ultrasound panels around my torso. I smiled when I saw the image of our child appear on the monitor. I looked at Nick to see his reaction, but his attention remained focused on his phone.

With someone else present, his disregard felt profound as the sound of our child's heartbeat filled the room. I was no longer able to lie to myself; his indifference was too painful to ignore. My doubts about uprooting my life were no longer whispers I could disregard but shouts of warning that blared through my ears. As I glared at him, only one question ran through my mind.

Why am I making his happiness more important than mine?

"Dad, what are you hoping for, a girl or a boy?" Dr. Solomon's whimsical voice asked.

"I'm just hoping for a healthy child," Nick responded with a cordial smile as he looked up for the first time.

"Well, that makes my job today very easy. Mom and Dad, congratulations! You are having a girl!"

Nick lowered his phone and stared at the monitor. He appeared transfixed by the image, but he didn't speak. Suddenly, without explanation, he excused himself from the room.

When the door closed, Dr. Solomon looked down at me with a puzzled look.

"Is Dad emotional?" she asked.

"Yes," I lied, embarrassed and equally confused by Nick's abrupt actions.

"Don't worry. It was a long time ago but my husband was the same way," she said though I suspected she was trying to make the moment less awkward.

I was able to get dressed after she recorded several images of the baby. She told me that she would see me in four more weeks. I collected my things and walked back into the waiting area where I saw Nick standing by the window, looking out onto the streets below.

Walking up behind him, I calmly organized my thoughts. If I said what I was thinking - *that he was far too selfish and self-absorbed to be anyone's father* – it would have surely resulted in an argument.

I didn't have the energy to fight with him, and I didn't want to say anything that I would regret. I was as hurt as I was confused, but I still needed to know what was wrong with him. I needed to know if becoming a father would be too much for him.

His thoughts seemed so far away that he didn't notice I was standing next to him until I tapped him on the shoulder.

"Lotus, I'm sorry," he said looking towards the floor. "I had to respond to something but, wow, a little girl, huh?"

I intended to be calm, but the fact that he couldn't look me in the eye infuriated me. Not confident that I would be able to say anything to him without yelling or crying, I turned and began to walk towards the elevator.

By the time we exited into the atrium together, my head throbbed with anger. I continued to walk ahead of him, afraid to begin a discussion while we were still in the hospital. It wasn't until I was almost at the door that I heard him calling after me. When I turned around to look for him, I saw him standing halfway across the room.

"What the hell is wrong with you? Why are you walking like you are insane?"

Walking towards him, I screamed back. "What the hell is wrong with me? What the hell is wrong with you?"

He grasped my arm and led me to a nearby bench. Once seated, neither of us said anything for a long time. It was obvious that we both had things that we needed to say to one another.

"What are we doing, Nick?" I asked, repositioning myself to look him directly in the eye. "It's time to be honest with me. Do you resent me for becoming pregnant? If you do, you don't have to stay in this marriage out of obligation. I will be okay. We will be okay, but I need to know."

As more silence followed, I braced myself for his response. As often as I had imagined asking him that question, my stomach was still in knots awaiting his answer. One part of me hoped that he would dismiss my question as completely ridiculous; another part of me wanted him to admit everything I had suspected.

"What exactly are you asking me, Lotus? You think you need to give me an out? I know I don't have to stay in this marriage out of obligation. Is that what you think I'm doing?"

All of the actions I had ignored and every emotion I had dismissed for five and a half months surfaced at once. Despite his offended response, I refused to believe that I had completely fabricated the idea that he may have wanted out of our marriage.

"I don't know how you feel, Nick, and that's the problem. I know that I shouldn't feel this alone. I know that the way you have responded to this pregnancy isn't right. I know what just happened in Dr. Solomon's office isn't normal. And, despite all of this, you expect me to transplant my life, our life, and our child's life to another country with you? Why would I do that when I feel like I have no support from you while we are still here?"

He interrupted, "Lotus, you don't understand."

"Then help me to understand because I feel completely lost."

"I am committed to you and our..."

"I don't believe you," I said.

"You don't believe me?" he said, rolling his eyes. "I think I've proven to you that there is nothing that I wouldn't do for you. Who do you think that I am working this hard for?"

He was incensed. "I can't believe that, after all this time, I still have to try to convince you of how I feel about you. If you don't know, it's not because I haven't shown you. I have never been able to convince you that I could truly love you."

People stared as they walked past us on the bench. I wished that we could continue the conversation somewhere else, but I feared that if we moved, we would both lose our nerve to be completely honest with each other.

"Marriage is about more than being a provider, Nick. I'm your wife, not your child. I married you because you were my best friend, but since the day I told you I was pregnant, you stopped being that and I deserve to know why."

Looking past him, I could see a middle-aged but burly-looking security guard walking towards us from across the room. I didn't know if it was the shine from his bald head or the way that his biceps flexed every time that he took a step, but if it wasn't for the words "SAFETY OFFICER" written across his chest, I would have easily mistaken him for the WWE wrestler John Cena.

"Don't try to convince me that your decision to focus more on your job than your marriage has been about us. And don't you dare try to convince me that going to Paris is more about me and this child than about your ambition," I said, quickly turning my attention back to Nick.

Once the security guard finally approached us, I tried to appear calm.

"Look, folks, arguments happen in this lobby more than people suspect. I just need you all to lower your voices, or I'm going to have to ask you to step outside," he said with an assertive nod before heading back across the room.

Nick agreed. "Let's go, Lotus. We can finish talking in the car on our way to Wisconsin."

He grabbed my arm, but I didn't budge. I wasn't going to move an inch until he explained what happened in Dr. Solomon's office.

"I'm not going anywhere until you tell me what is wrong. What could have been so important that you had to leave in the middle of finding out the gender of your child?"

Even with the exhausted look in his eyes, I could see the wheels turning in his head. I waited for him to respond.

After what felt like an eternity, a look of resolve crossed his face.

"I already said yes to the fellowship. I already accepted the offer."

His lips were moving but after his first words I could no longer hear anything that he said. Everything around us seemed to slow down as I tried to process what I just heard him say. Every conversation we had about the fellowship since December flipped through my mind. As he continued to speak, I replayed every discussion we had about making the decision together.

"When did you accept the offer?" I asked, unable to look him in the eye. A nauseated feeling swept through my stomach.

"Lotus."

"Answer my question, please, Nick. When did you accept the offer?" I asked again though I already knew the answer.

"I accepted it the day I received it," he said without looking at me. "We had talked about the fellowship for months and we had talked about moving if I got it. There was no reason to think that I wouldn't be able to accept it. I've been trying to figure out how to tell you ever since."

Everything around me faded into the background and Nick was the only thing that I could see. My mind didn't race; my thoughts were suddenly crystal clear.

"You've lied to me for months? You pretended to consider staying, but rather than to tell me the truth, you chose to manipulate me until I felt guilted into going? Instead of making me your partner in this decision, you fabricated a non-choice to get what you wanted. Because you were sure that no matter what, I would choose you over any uncertainties that I had, right?"

"Lotus," he said. He reached out to grab my arm again, but I pulled away from him before he could touch me.

"Answer my question."

"No," he said, looking away from me again. "I mean yes. I assumed that you would eventually see that Paris is the best decision for all of us. I'm not going to lie about that. You hate your career, and there's nothing to keep us from going. You've known since we first met that this was my dream. I've given up a lot for our marriage, and I didn't want to have to give this up, too. There isn't a real reason you shouldn't be willing to go."

"So you assumed that this was the least I could do in return for everything that you've done for me, right?" I said, cutting him off.

"The sad thing is that I used to believe that, too. I convinced myself that what you have put into our relationship has been more valuable that what I have. Now I know that's complete bullshit because you have no idea what I've walked away from because of my love for you."

"That's not what I am saying," Nick yelled.

I could hear bystanders whispering as they walked past us, and I could see the looks on peoples' faces wondering if they should intervene. I slid closer to Nick, but I couldn't bear to look him in the eye.

"I've seen your sacrifices, Nick. I considered them acts of love even though you have dismissed my sacrifices as mere retribution.

I'm sorry, but I'm not willing to eat a pile of hot steaming shit and raise our child in another country because of some miscalculated debt that you envision that I owe you."

I saw the security guard walking back towards us from across the room. Nick must have noticed him too because he immediately stood up and made an effort to appear less angry than he obviously was.

"Lotus, can we please talk about this in the car?" he asked again, nodding towards the man walking towards us.

"No, Nick, we can't talk about this in the car," I said coldly. "I don't want to be near you right now and I need to clear my mind. I'll just see you back at home." I gathered my things and stood.

He called after me as I headed towards the hospital exit, but I didn't turn around. I wasn't sure if our relationship would ever be the same.

SIXTEEN

"Take the jacket, Lotus, you're shaking," Gabe demanded from the other side of the table.

It was the first time I'd seen him in an outfit other than hospital scrubs since Layla's funeral. If it weren't for the few gray hairs in his beard, he could easily pass for a student in his button-up shirt and blazer. I hadn't considered the possibility of him not being at work when I sent him a text asking if he was able to meet me. I only knew that I needed to talk to someone who wouldn't judge me for how I felt.

When he arrived at the table, we acknowledged each other with a smile. He sat down without saying anything as I tried quickly to piece together what I wanted to say. Even though every part of my brain knew that he was the last person I needed to see, I also realized that any remaining feelings between us needed to be dissolved if my marriage was to survive.

I had walked aimlessly for hours after leaving the hospital, resisting my default response to call Lola or Dakota. I had no doubt that both of them would have reminded me of how willing I said I would be to move to Paris. They would have also tried to convince me that Nick's actions weren't horrible enough to reconsider going. Even if they were right, they weren't the ones who were expected to uproot their lives and raise a child with someone who they weren't sure they could trust.

Gabe didn't say much after offering me his coat. The small café where we met was nested on the busy end of Oak Street, so the noise from the traffic on the boulevard filled the silence between us. When I glanced in his direction, he smiled at me hesitantly. Still unsure of where to begin, I smiled back and took hold of one of his hands, which were resting on the table.

"Happy birthday," he said.

"Thank you."

We continued to sit in silence watching the people on the street. With each person who walked past the window, my thoughts became clearer. I understood why Gabe was the perfect person to have there with me, in light of everything that had just happened. Regardless of all the years that had passed since we were together, I knew that he wouldn't lie to me. At that moment, honesty was what I needed the most.

"I assumed you would be at work when I texted you. I hope you didn't have to come far to meet me."

"I don't have to be there until this evening, and I actually live about five blocks away," he said, pointing past me in the direction of a cluster of high rise buildings.

Seeing our server approaching our table, I fumbled with the menu though I wasn't hungry. Trying to scan the sandwich options as quickly as I could, I sensed the waitress growing impatient.

"Let's start with two chamomile teas - one with honey and lemon, the other with honey and milk. Once those come out we will figure out if we want something to eat," Gabe offered.

His blazer was wrapped around my shoulders, but I felt the instant prick of goose bumps developing on my arms. I had begun to drink my tea with milk and honey while in London, but it was difficult to imagine how he remembered such a random detail over ten years later.

Once the waitress left us, silence returned to our table. Not wanting to waste any more time, I began to tell Gabe about the argument I had with Nick.

"Would you go?" I asked after telling him everything.

He took a sip of tea and laughed.

"That's a very loaded question, Lotus. For starters, I haven't made a vow to stay with someone for the rest of my life, and I'm not pregnant. I'm probably not the best person to ask," he said with a hint of sarcasm in his voice.

"I'm serious, Gabe."

"I know you are," he said as he looked down at his cup of tea uncomfortably.

I recognized that it was selfish of me to talk to him about Nick, but after everything he had said to me, I felt like he owed me this conversation. My faith in his honesty trumped my need for either of us to be comfortable. If I had overreacted, I had no doubt that he would tell me so. If my distrust in my husband was warranted, I believed that he would tell me that as well. Unlike Nick, who constantly saw it as his duty to protect me from myself, Gabe wasn't the type to spare my feelings. Since the day we first met, he had a way of showing me things about myself that I may not have wanted to acknowledge.

"Do you think that I am unreasonable?" I asked.

"Maybe," he said flatly.

"Do you think I'm hypocritical?"

"Perhaps."

His eyes shifted away from me and back towards the people on the street. It was obvious that he wanted to avoid continuing the conversation, but I pressed him to finish speaking.

"You are going to have to give me more than that," I said.

"Your feelings may be hurt but being manipulated isn't the worst thing that can happen in a relationship. It's bound to happen in any marriage. At least he thought he was doing it for the benefit of your relationship."

"I'm not so sure that's why he did it," I said.

"Your husband wanted to find a way to live his dream with you in it. I would be a liar if I told you that I could fault him for that."

The waitress arrived back at our table and replenished our water. After taking a sip and thinking about what he said, I found myself feeling guilty about everything – the argument at the hospital, not trusting Nick's intentions, and having lunch with a man whom I continued to love.

As if he were reading my mind, Gabe continued.

"But I think you need to be honest with yourself. The reason we're having this conversation is not because of what Nick did, it's because you still don't know if moving to Paris is something that you want to do. It's less about him manipulating you and more about the fact that you are still looking for an out. As much as you may want to paint yourself as a martyr, not telling your husband that you simply don't want to move makes you just as dishonest as he has been."

His sudden curtness caught me by surprise. I was embarrassed because he was right. Even if Gabe hadn't reentered my life, I would be leery of spending the first several years of my child's life away from the people and things that have supported me the most.

"You would have been able to accept the decision as long as you were the one to make it under the guise of self-sacrifice. Sooner or later you would have thought he was selfish because he didn't fall on the sword that you set out for yourself. So you didn't want to decide the outcome with him; you wanted to control who would be seen as the good guy versus the bad guy."

There was a hint of anger in his voice that was difficult to miss. We were no longer just talking about Nick and me.

"I'm just scared," I whispered under my breath.

"I know."

"Regardless of what decision I make, I'm about to have a child whom I will end up raising alone. If I'm in Paris, I will be alone because work will consume Nick. If I stay here, then my family would be destroyed before it began. I am going to have regrets regardless of what decision I make."

"You wouldn't be alone if you stayed," Gabe said.

"I'll have Lola and Dakota, but I don't want to depend on them to help me raise my child. I don't want to raise my child apart her father."

"That's not what I meant," he interrupted.

I stared at him. He knew what I wanted to ask him, but I didn't have the nerve to take our conversation any further.

"Lotus, I'm trying to be as respectful as I can to your husband, but my feelings haven't changed. I've waited a very long time to be able to tell you again that I love you, and I want you. No matter what. I will be here as long as you need me to be. I need you to tell me that you want me to be here. I need for you to decide if you want to be with me."

Stunned at his proposition, thoughts of the mistakes and happiness of our past overcame me like an avalanche. I wasn't able to fully process what he was suggesting, but I did know that I wasn't ready to walk away from my marriage.

"I don't know what I want right now."

"I know and that's why I'm asking you to figure it out."

"What about your fiancée?"

"I told you before. She's not you."

"That tells me nothing."

"It means that if you asked me to leave her then I would leave. It means that if you don't want to go to Paris you don't have to because I would be here for you."

"...and what happens if I decide to go?" I asked him reluctantly.

"If you decide to leave then I would have to force myself to let you go."

SEVENTEN

I tiptoed through the hallway so softly that if any of my neighbors had opened their doors they would have thought that I was breaking into my home. Unsure of whether Nick was there or not, I held my breath as I twisted the doorknob. Once I entered the hallway and realized that I was alone, I exhaled, relieved.

During the taxi ride home, I had thought about the day Nick proposed. It was one of the few times in my life I had been truly surprised even though we had dated for more than four years. I loved him, but he knew that I was in no rush to get married because the idea of planning for something that is supposed to last forever petrified me.

I adored him, but I was leery of needing him, and he accepted that about me. Instead of trying to break down the wall that I had built around myself, he tasked himself with protecting it. I loved him for that. He accepted that he was going to spend the rest of his life with the sort of woman who was always preparing for the other shoe to drop. Over the years, I wondered if that hurt his feelings but I had had no idea until our argument at the hospital that it ever did.

The condo was illuminated only by the dim light of the sun setting over the lake. Feeling mentally and physically exhausted, I went out onto the balcony to sit. The warmth of the breeze coming off the water was calming so I closed my eyes and forced myself to relax.

My thoughts began to oscillate between Nick and Gabe. After leaving Gabe, I sat at a small park for hours, hoping to make sense of what was happening. I tried to dismiss the anger that I felt towards Nick. I wanted to forget everything that Gabe said to me at the end of our lunch, but I couldn't. Thinking of my child, I knew that I owed it to her to keep the vows that I made with Nick, if I possibly could. That was more important to me than anything else.

The warm breeze that was coming off the lake had strengthened. Though I could tell that it was going to rain, I didn't move. My eyes became entranced by the lights on the sailboats floating at a distance until I let go of my vying thoughts and drifted to sleep.

***

I woke up to the sound of the fireworks show at Navy Pier. Realizing that it had to be after 10:00 o'clock, I turned around to see that the lights throughout the house were still off. I walked through the house without making a sound, assuming that Nick had slipped in while I was sleeping and was already in our bedroom. When I opened the door to peek in, I was surprised to see that he wasn't there. The only reminder of his presence was his laptop and messenger bag lying on our bed.

I began to worry after checking my phone for messages. Even if he had gone to his office on campus, there was no reason for him not to be home yet. Considering the magnitude of our fight, I resisted the impulse to call him and decided to stay up until he got home. Not wanting to make things between us any worse, I resolved to spend the rest of the night on the couch, watching old movies and playing spider solitaire until he arrived so we could talk.

I changed into the only nightgown that was both clean and unpacked, and grabbed Nick's laptop before heading back into the living room. After making some popcorn and a root beer float, I settled into my favorite corner of our couch. Famished, I stuffed a handful of kernels in my mouth before I opened his laptop to see an email that had been left open. I moved the mouse to close to the window. My hand stopped short when I saw the subject line, *8:30 at our sports bar.*

I was slightly relieved to have an idea of where he was, but a feeling in my gut told me not to close the message. I pulled up the chain of emails between Nick and the recipient, which revealed a long thread of peer reviews, articles and workshop agendas. Piecing together that the person on the email was a coworker, my unease began to lift until I came to the last email.

Sorry about Wisconsin. Would love to hook up. Call me when you are on your way.
Yours,
Brooke

I sat on the couch running through several explanations for the email. Each time I reread it, my heart pounded harder. Each time I skimmed the words, my attention would come back to the one word that I couldn't dismiss as insignificant.

Yours

I checked my phone again to see if Nick had texted or called me. After seeing he hadn't, I couldn't deny that something was obviously wrong. Feeling sick to my stomach, I knew that I wouldn't be able to think clearly waiting for him in the house, so I grabbed my raincoat and left.

***

I drove to every bar near his campus and eventually found myself outside a sports bar that Nick had once mentioned going to with friends. Praying that I was insanely hormonal and paranoid, I parked across from it and checked my phone, hoping to see that I missed a call from him. When I saw that I hadn't, I settled into my seat and watched people stream in and out.

Every time the door rotated, I thought about every early morning meeting, every late night and every Saturday when

Nick had said he had to go to his office. A picture began to come together in my mind of all the opportunities Nick had for indiscretions and I wondered if he had been betraying me in plain sight. Unable to accept that I had missed so many signs that he could be cheating, I reminded myself of one of the first things I learned in law school, suspicion isn't proof of a person's wrongdoing.

Staring at drunken sports fans leaving the bar, I began to feel ridiculous. I was angry with myself for letting my guilt make me think the worst about Nick and decided to return home.

He is probably at home asleep, I thought.

I prepared to drive off as a group of college students headed to the bar abruptly crossed in front of my car. My gaze followed them as they crossed the street until my eyes caught a glimpse of Nick walking out of the bar with a woman.

My heart sank when I saw him laughing. Shocked, I reclined back into my seat and watched them as they walked slowly down the street together. When he stopped to steady himself, I realized that he was drunk. He continued to laugh and stumble backward towards the street. The woman he was with lingered close to him as he swayed from side to side. She whispered in his ear as he reached for the bottle of water that was in her hand.

Watching them laugh, I couldn't remember the last time he looked that happy. I considered getting out the car, but resisted out of fear of what would happen if I confronted them. I was satisfied with spying on them from afar until I saw Nick lower his face to hers, and the woman put her arms around his waist.

I jumped out of my car without thinking and ran across the street in their direction until I was out of breath. Realizing that they were too far ahead for me to catch up with them, I screamed Nick's name at the top of my lungs. He turned around and looked down the street in my direction.

"Lotus?" he yelled back with a drunken lisp.

The woman he was with backed away from him and her hands began to wave at me dismissively.

"This isn't what you think," she said loud enough for me to hear as she began to walk towards me.

Nick's pace quickened behind her. Once he was close enough for me to hit him, I threw my car keys at his face as hard as I could.

"Lotus!" the woman interjected.

I was caught off guard by her familiarity with me. Before I could ask who she was, she pulled her phone out of her purse and began to punch numbers that I instantly recognized.

Once Nick caught up with us, I saw horror in his eyes. Confused for a second, I followed his eyes to the bottom of my gown. It was covered with blood.

EIGHTEEN

The sight of him repulsed me. I couldn't hear much over the sound of the sirens, but I didn't care that I was being driven to Lakeshore Medical's Emergency Room. All I could think about was her. The blood that still stained my hands and my nightgown was a reminder that nothing meant more to me at that moment than my daughter's life.

Every time I felt the stroke of his hand on my head I was disgusted. Since the paramedics had arrived, I could do nothing but lie motionless and pray that I would hear her heartbeat again. I didn't bother resisting his touch; I just closed my eyes and waited. I didn't bother to wipe the tears that poured down my face; each one felt like rightful punishment for everything Nick and I had done to each other.

He leaned over me and said something. I opened my eyes to follow the outline of his lips until I deciphered the words I'M SORRY coming from his mouth over and over again.

Turning away, I closed my eyes and was back in a self-imposed darkness. I ignored the murmurings of his voice beside me and tried to envision her face. I tried to imagine holding her in my arms and what her voice would one day sound like. Imagining if she would have freckles like me and my sisters, I thought of Layla and whispered aloud.

"Layla, if you are there please help."

As I was rushed through the ER, I didn't hear anything. The voices of Nick and the nurses who surrounded me were muffled by the white noise in my head. I was taken immediately to a room where a barrage of people rotated in and out. Within minutes, my entire body was connected to various monitors and machines as I waited for someone to tell me something.

From across the room, I could see Nick pacing in the corner, frantically talking to someone on the phone. Making out the words LOLA, PLANE, and MORNING FLIGHT, I assumed that he was speaking with my parents, who now lived in Arizona. Worried that they would hear that I was brought to the same emergency room where Layla died, I began to blame myself again for everything that was happening.

Nurses continued to come in and out of the room. After quickly greeting me, each of them spoke to Nick at greater length. Unable to hear what was being said, I removed my oxygen mask to demand that someone explain to me what was happening.

Before I could say a word, one of the nurses reprimanded me and quickly placed it back over my face.

"We need to ensure that you are getting enough oxygen. Your heart rate is elevated, and that's not good for your baby."

I felt helpless. The only thing I could do to help my child was to accept that there was nothing that I could do to save her. I closed my eyes and tried to search for any sign within me that she was still there. I searched for a movement, anything that would let me know that she was okay, but again I felt nothing.

Unable to sense her presence, it felt like the air was slowly being pulled from my chest. In a panic, I frantically began to pull at the cords attached to my body until the mask on my face finally fell off again. Nick rushed to my side as alarms from the machines around me began to blare. One of the nurses in the room tried to calm me, but I was inconsolable.

Nick walked to the side of the bed and reached for my hand. I was too scared to push him away. The clamminess of his palm was a sobering reminder that I wasn't dreaming. Just as the nurses began to reattach the various lobes to my body, Gabe entered the room with another doctor.

He glanced at Nick but didn't acknowledge him. His eyes locked with mine as the other doctor briefed him on details of my medical situation. The worry in his eyes was evident though he tried his best to mask it. Once they were finished speaking, Gabe, and the woman who entered with him walked over to my bed.

Even with Nick holding on to my hand, I began to cry again.

"Hi, Lotus," he said.

The spaces that lingered between his greeting and his next words were almost too long. I caught probing glances flash across the faces of the other people surrounding us before Gabe continued.

"My name is Dr. Lincoln and I will be overseeing your care. In a moment, we will be doing an ultrasound, but I need to know if you are in any physical pain right now?"

I shook my head to signal that I was not.

"Have you felt any contractions?"

I shook my head again.

"Great, that means that we are off to a very good start. One of my residents will perform the ultrasound while I press gently on your abdomen. If you feel pain at any time, I need for you to tell me immediately, okay?"

I nodded my head affirmatively.

His resident took Gabe's place beside me. As I saw Gabe walking to the other side of the bed where Nick stood, the monitor that tracked my heart rate began to bing loudly.

"Mrs. Price, please try your best to relax," the other doctor beside me said.

"She's okay," Gabe replied before turning to Nick.

"Sir, I need to take your place," he said with a fleeting smile that only I caught. "You can have a seat in that chair until we are done."

Once Nick was behind him, Gabe whispered, "I promise I won't let anything happen to you or your baby."

The resident pulled my nightgown above my torso to reveal my stomach. Feeling both scared and self-conscious, I closed my eyes. Despite the coolness of the medical gel on my stomach, I still flinched when I felt the warmth of Gabe's hands. As he gently pressed along the sides of my stomach, I held my breath, waiting to see or hear something.

It felt like an eternity before anyone in the room spoke. The doctors moved the orbs along the middle of my body in different directions. My heart pounded painfully in my chest until they finally stopped. When I opened my eyes, I saw Gabe looking at me with a slight smile.

"Look at the monitor. The sound is muted but that's your baby. Heart rate and vitals look good. Your little one is fine."

I began to cry uncontrollably and was grateful that my wails were muffled by the mask on my face. Nick broke into tears as he sat back into his chair. Gabe instructed the younger doctor to arrange to have me transferred to the Intensive Care Unit for further testing and overnight observation.

"It looks like your bleeding was caused by a condition called placenta previa. In most pregnancies, the placenta attaches to the top or side of the uterus but in your case the placenta is on the bottom, partially covering your cervix. Though this is what is causing the bleeding, from the position of it, I think that it will likely to correct itself – and move upwards away from your cervix – by the time you are to deliver."

"Will she need to be put on bed rest?" Nick asked from across the room.

Gabe hesitated before he responded. For the first time, he looked at Nick directly.

"At this point I'm going to say no. We are going to conduct another ultrasound in the morning to get a better understanding of how low-lying the placenta currently is. After that, we will recommend that Lotus follows up with her obstetrician who will likely recommend that she just abstain from any strenuous physical activities."

"So no exercising?" Nick asked.

"More like no sex," Gabe answered.

Turning his attention back to me, Gabe smirked.

"So traveling would be out of the question as well, I'm assuming?"

From the look on Gabe's face I could see that he was just as dumbfounded as I when Nick asked the question. His silence made the mood in the room instantly uncomfortable. I was too stunned by Nick's nerve to try to interject.

"I think that decision is best left to your wife and her doctor."

Sensing Gabe's judgment, Nick retreated. "Thanks, Doctor. That makes sense."

"I have to see another patient, but please let the nurses know if you need anything. You will be transferred to the ICU, but I'll be sure to tell your nurses to page me personally if anything comes up."

He motioned for his resident to follow him out. Moments later, the nurses were out of the room, and only Nick and I remained.

He walked to the bed. Before I could resist, he grabbed my hand and held it tightly over his chest.

"Please let me explain what happened."

Still unable to speak through my oxygen mask, I lifted it off of my face.

"Lotus."

"Wait, let me speak," I interrupted him. "Nick, less than five minutes ago I thought that I was having a miscarriage. Earlier today, I found out that you have been lying to me for almost six months. An hour ago, I saw you kissing another woman. After all of that, the only thing you're still concerned with is whether or not I am going to Paris with you? After everything that has happened, do you really think that I would still go with you?"

The look of confusion on his face made me realize that it was the first time that he considered the possibility that I wouldn't.

"Lotus, you have to let me explain everything. I understand why you are upset, but you can't just make this decision without letting me explain."

"I just did, Nick," I said not recognizing the coldness in my voice.

When I heard the sequence of beeps on the monitors around me, I knew I only had a few seconds to finish saying what it was that I needed to say.

Physically and emotionally exhausted, I took his hand and pulled him towards me. I could still smell the cognac that he had been drinking on his breath as I pulled his ear to my mouth.

"Nick, I love you, but I do not want you here. The best thing you can do for me, our child, and our marriage right now is to leave us alone."

NINETEEN

DECEMBER 2009

"Lotus, do you want to come to the movies with us?" Lola asked, unable to hide the concern in her voice.

I didn't respond. I wasn't ignoring her, but I assumed that my silence would answer her question. Since Layla died, I hadn't spoken more than three words to anyone, including her.

My parents worried that I was having a mental breakdown, though Lola continually assured them that I would be okay. She explained that it wasn't that I could not speak but that I had disconnected myself from everything around me. Every time someone would try to engage me in a conversation, I felt paralyzed and numb. After I spending days locked in my apartment, Lola insisted that I come stay at her house. Two weeks later, I was still sleeping on her couch, afraid of going anywhere else.

Every time her home phone rang, I feared the worst. Every time she and her husband left the house with my niece and nephew, I worried that they wouldn't return. I knew I needed to talk to someone, but my entire family was steeped in their grief. Instead of admitting to anyone the guilt that I felt over Layla's death, I retreated more into myself with each day that passed.

Memories that ranged from her first date to the first half marathon we ran together continually drifted through my mind. I repeatedly called my voicemail to listen to her last message. Each time I heard her say that she was waiting for me for our weekly run, feelings of regret swept over me. The guilt of wondering if she would still be alive if I had gotten to her apartment on time had plagued me since the day she died.

"No, I'm okay," I responded.

I continued to hold onto my three-year-old niece, Eden, who had been sitting in my lap for the past hour. After finishing *Toy Story*, she cued *Finding Nemo* in the DVD player. As the opening credits came on, I was grateful that another day was almost over. Just as I began to relax, my niece hopped off of the couch and ran to my sister who was watching us from her stairway.

"No more movies, Auntie Lolo! Mommy, can I go to Grammy's house?"

"Okay, sweetie, come upstairs so you can get dressed," she said as she began to climb the stairs with Eden in tow. "I'll call Grammy to see if she will watch you while Daddy and I go to the movies. That'll give your Auntie Lolo a little time to herself."

Feeling abandoned by my niece, I pulled the blanket that we had shared for the past few hours over my head. Thinking about the Legal Ethics final exam that I was scheduled to take the following morning, I considered emailing my professor for an extension but decided against it. Even with one semester left of law school, the possibility of failing wasn't enough to motivate me to move from Lola's couch.

An hour later, my sister and her family made a grand exodus from the house. When I heard the door shut behind them, the house immediately felt painfully desolate. Uncomfortable with its silence, I flipped through an endless number of channels that seemed to be playing only romantic comedies and football games. I succumbed to watching an hour of *Breakfast at Tiffany's* before I turned the television off and decided to stop putting off the inevitable.

Grudgingly, I made a quick sweep through the hundreds of emails I had avoided for the past two weeks. As I suspected, most of them were about Layla. Abandoning the effort to respond to any of them, I looked through my inbox one last time. There was only one email that I was hoping to see, but deep down I already knew that it wasn't there.

I caught a glimpse of Gabe at Layla's funeral though he avoided eye contact with me when I noticed him. As I spoke Layla's eulogy in front of my family and her friends, his face was the only one I saw. Waiting in the limo to go to the cemetery, I searched the crowd of people leaving the church, but he was nowhere to be found. I considered emailing him to thank him for coming, but each time I tried, I stopped short.

Looking down, the sight of the tattered Harvard t-shirt I had been wearing for the past week was suddenly sobering. Remembering that he broke up with me with a letter and a t-shirt, I forced myself to put his lack of communication into perspective. Despite our exchange in the hospital, it was useless to expect to hear from him. He would never allow himself to be uncomfortable long enough to face any feelings that remained between us from our past.

I tried to purge him from my mind, but I instantly saw a snapshot of Layla's face. I thought about the conversation we had while on vacation in Maui, only five months earlier. I wished she was there so badly that my heart felt like it was going to break in half. Feeling more alone than ever, I decided to go to the one place I had avoided since she died because it was also the place where I would feel the closest to her.

***

She had been in the middle of her third year of undergrad at the University of Chicago, so word of her passing spread quickly. Though the law school was on the other side of campus, it took less than a day before my classmates and professors began to bombard me with emails, texts, and calls. Even though finals had just begun, I had managed to avoid campus for almost three weeks. I knew once I returned I would be faced with a barrage of condolences and well-intentioned questions that I didn't have the strength to answer.

After driving around campus for a place to study, I ended up at the university's Regenstein Library. As a classical studies major, the massive building had been one of Layla's favorite places on campus. Luckily for me, the sheer volume of its stacks also made it the perfect place for someone to hide out. But it wasn't long after walking through the doors that I regretted my choice.

I flashed my student ID at the registration counter and headed for the stairs on the main floor. Just as I made it to the first landing, I recognized a tall, red-haired girl walking down the stairs towards me. I tried to avoid her by looking away, but it was too late.

As soon as we met on the second landing, she embraced me in a hug. In tears, she reminded me that she and Layla were both in the Classical Lecture Society together and recounted how kind Layla had been to her when she first joined. Accepting there was no way to end our conversation without appearing rude, I spent five minutes consoling her as best as I could. Once we finally parted ways, I walked up the remaining stairs as fast as I could and looked for the first available study room.

As soon as I closed the door, the walls felt like they were closing in on me. In an instant, my entire body was drenched with sweat and my eyes couldn't focus. Afraid, I tried to call Lola but when I got her voicemail, I remembered that she was at the movies.

Leaving everything behind, I rushed out of the room. It wasn't until I was back in the cold air that I felt like I wasn't going to die. Trying my best to hold back my tears, I found a bench in the library's courtyard and buried my head between my knees.

"You don't call. You don't write. Was I really that bad in bed?"

Even before I looked up, my heart sank deeper into my chest. Despite the smile on his face, I knew that his feelings were genuinely hurt.

Just three weeks before I had wondered if I might love him. Even though we had only been dating for a few months, I imagined that if things were different, I could spend the rest of my life with him. With only weeks remaining until he defended his dissertation, I saw him less frequently than I had become accustomed. Though we had been dating for months, I still refused to call him my boyfriend because I knew that our lives were headed in starkly different directions.

"Nick. I'm sorry. It's finals, and things have been busy for me," I lied, avoiding eye contact with him.

To my relief, he obviously hadn't heard about Layla, and I didn't want to tell him. If I began to explain what happened to her, then it wouldn't take much for him to figure out that I had been with him the morning that she died. After sleeping together for the first time, he spent the morning trying to convince me to spend the rest of the weekend with him at his apartment. I didn't want him to know the details of Layla's death because I knew he would feel responsible, which was not what I wanted.

"It's finals? Wow," he said. "That's a bit cold, even for you, Lotus. Did I piss you off and not realize it?"

I felt horrible, but I didn't have the energy to focus on his hurt feelings. I prepared myself to tell him that I needed some space when I saw a younger guy on a bike riding towards us.

The dread I felt as the boy neared us must have been apparent because Nick immediately turned around.

"What's wrong?" he said, appearing worried.

Before I could respond, the boy approached us and told me that he was at Layla's funeral. He went on to explain that he had seen Layla the morning that she died, and a look of recognition spread across Nick's face. When the boy finally walked away, we stood there in silence, neither of us knowing what to say.

"The last time I saw you..." I began.

"Stop, you don't have to explain right now," he interrupted.

He wrapped me inside his coat where I buried my head and began to cry again. I wanted to apologize for not telling him earlier, but I felt that he understood.

"I'm so sorry," he said.

"You didn't do anything, Nick. It hurts to imagine what she went through that morning, but I don't believe anything could have changed what happened."

"But I'm still sorry," he said, and the regret that he felt was evident in his tone. "Do you need anything? Is there anything that I can do?"

"I just need for you to be here," I uncomfortably admitted. "But I don't want you to feel obligated or like I expect anything from you. I know you have other priorities."

"What is that supposed to mean?" he asked, obviously hurt.

"Look, Nick, we can be honest. In a few months, you will probably be running a microfinance program in Sri Lanka or another third world country. I will probably be working 65 hours a week at a corporate law firm. I know you would want to be here for me, but life has other plans for you."

He kissed me on my forehead. "You are wrong. I am here now, and plans can change. If you need me, you should know that there's no part of me that I would ever keep from you."

TWENTY

"Will the baby be able to hear my Happy Birthday *sthong*, Auntie Lolo?" Eden asked with her endearing trademark lisp.

Looking at her in the outfit that she picked out for her party, she reminded me of myself when I was nine years old. Her eclectic assemble consisted of a pink skirt, striped purple tights and an emerald green shirt that made perfect sense in a weird sort of way. She had a small gap between her front two teeth which seemed to make her bright smile even cuter. The freckles she inherited from my sister covered her cheeks, and our family's trademark curly strands messily topped her head. Even though she was far from womanhood, I couldn't help but think of how mature she had become since the last time I was a houseguest in Lola's home, nearly six years ago.

Before I could think of a charming answer to her question, she was distracted by another thought.

"Guess what, Auntie Lolo?" she asked, luring me into her favorite game.

"What?" I responded, anticipating one of her trademark chicken-crossing-the-road jokes.

"I get my doggie today!" she shrieked, grinning from ear to ear.

"Oh, really? So you finally got your mom and dad to give in?" I asked, winking at Lola as she brushed Eden's hair into a ponytail.

"No! Not Mommy and Daddy! Uncle Nick is bringing her to my party!" she screamed as she began to bounce up and down with excitement. "Do you know what kind of dog she is?"

I unintentionally ignored her question because I was busy glaring at Lola, who was trying her best to appear oblivious to the conversation that we were having. I hadn't seen Nick since the day I was discharged from the hospital, nearly a week ago. He called to check on me twice a day, but I kept our conversations brief. Though we had an innumerable amount of issues that needed to be resolved, I made the decision to focus only on myself and the baby for the immediate future.

I needed time to sort through everything that had happened over the past six months and didn't want to be forced into a reconciliation that I wasn't ready for. Lola of all people should have understood that.

Lola wrapped a pink feather boa around Eden's neck to complete my niece's one-of-a-kind look. Eden twirled around twice in front of us before striking a pose in front of the long mosaic mirror that stood in the corner of her room. Just as we both gave her a thumbs-up, the doorbell rang.

"Ask your father to go with you to answer the door," Lola yelled as Eden ran full speed out the room towards the stairway.

Once I was sure that she was out of our earshot, I turned to Lola.

"When were you going to tell me that you invited Nick?" I asked.

"What do you mean when was I going to tell you? Nick was invited, with you, a month ago when the invitations went out to everyone. Besides, Eden told Nick at the hospital that he couldn't come to the party or see you unless he brought her a dog for her birthday."

Though the thought of Eden blackmailing Nick made me laugh, I still had a feeling that Lola was trying to force my hand. Over the past week, she had numerous opportunities to tell me that Nick was coming to the house, but she hadn't said a word.

"You didn't think it would be a good idea to give me a heads up?" I asked.

Lola turned towards me and took a deep breath. From the look on her face, I could tell that she was irritated with me.

"Lotus, Nick is your husband and you need to talk to him. I love you, but you can't hide out in my house forever. You are married and being married means that you work through issues together, regardless of how ugly the process might be. You can't hide out here for weeks on end, as you did six years ago, just because you don't want to face what's going on in your life," she said as she walked past me towards her room.

"I'm not trying to hide from anything, Lola," I yelled after her, following her down the hallway. "But I do think that I should be able to deal with my situations in my own time, and in the manner that I think is best. Call me crazy, but I don't recall asking you to orchestrate anything regarding my marriage on my behalf."

It was rare that I stood up to Lola, in part because she embodies every bit of our mother's intimidating assertiveness. When she stopped walking midway down the hall, I was sure that she was going to tell me that I could pack my things and leave.

"Look, Lotus, I support you no matter what you decide," she said, softening her tone. "But you need to talk to your husband. Remember, it's no longer just about you," she said before walking into her room and closing the door.

When I walked back into her guestroom alone, I thought about what she said. I had been avoiding Nick, and it wasn't only because of things that he had done. The truth was that I thought about Gabe's proposition as much as I thought about whether Nick and I could save our marriage. The only conclusion that I had come to is that I needed to avoid them both, as long as I could.

The doorbell rang again, and seconds later I heard the sound of a barking puppy. My suspicion of Nick's arrival was confirmed when I heard Eden scream, "Thank you, Uncle Nick! I love her so much already!"

I got up from the bed and quickly glanced in the mirror to check my appearance. Though I hadn't planned on it, the yellow chiffon sundress I was wearing happened to be one of Nick's favorites. Forcing myself to be open to having a face-to-face conversation with him, I slipped on my favorite pair of ballet flats and headed down the stairs.

A few minutes later, I stepped into the backyard where Eden and a few of her friends had already begun to play.

As I stood in front of the doors leading into the yard, I saw Nick and Michael explaining safety rules to the kids for playing with the bite-sized Cavalier King Charles Spaniel. It was difficult to tell if the kids were listening or not because they all continuously yelled reasons why they should be the first to hold the puppy. Predictably, Eden eventually grabbed the small puppy from Nick and ran off to the wooden swing in the middle of the yard with all ten of her friends in tow.

Looking at Nick with Eden and her friends, I tried to imagine what type of father he might be with our daughter. Would she see him as her protector as I did my father, or would she only see him as a distant provider? Would he love her enough to put her ahead of his work? Could he assure her that he would always be there for her no matter what? My anxiety must have been apparent because when he looked in my direction he looked concerned. As he began to walk towards the house, I couldn't help but smile. Deep down, even if I didn't want to admit it, I had missed seeing his face.

"Are you okay?" he asked once we met in the doorway.

"Yes, how are you?" I asked, noticing the heavy stubble growing on his usually clean-shaven face.

"I miss you," he blurted out, looking insecure in a way that I had never seen. "Can we go somewhere and talk?"

"Now?" I asked, looking out towards Eden and her friends in the yard.

"Yes, and don't worry because I already asked Eden if she would let you leave for a little while. She said that I could have you for the rest of the day, as long as we were back in time to see her blow out her candles."

I looked back at Eden, who was now showing her puppy to my mother, who had been back in town since I left the hospital. When she glanced in our direction she gave me an exaggerated wink and a thumbs up, as if she knew exactly what we were talking about.

"Since Eden has sold me out, it doesn't look like I have much of a choice," I said.

He held out his hand, and reluctantly I placed mine in his. A sense of comfort and familiarity instantly washed through me. As we headed to the door, Lola was coming down the stairs. I gave her a leery glance, and she smiled knowingly.

"Cake and candles will be at 5:00 o'clock so that should give you all about three hours."

As soon as we got into Nick's convertible, he dropped the top, which was something that he never did. Afraid of what it was going to do to my hair, I wanted to protest but resisted.

"It's a beautiful day. Let's try to enjoy it," he said as he veered down Lola's driveway and back to the main road.

After we'd been driving for fifteen minutes, I still had no idea where we were going. I had been to Evanston enough times to know where all the main restaurants were located, but we were going in the opposite direction. Out of habit, I reached for my phone but realized that I had left my purse at the house.

"Don't worry, you won't need it," Nick yelled as we turned down a road that I didn't recall seeing before.

"Where are we going?" I asked, but he pretended that he didn't hear me. It wasn't until I caught a glimpse of a tall tower through the trees that I pieced together where we were.

"Now do you remember?" Nick asked.

I nodded my head to acknowledge that I did. I didn't recognize the road leading to the lighthouse because the last time we were there, almost four years ago, it had been at night.

After parking the car, he went into his trunk and reemerged with a picnic basket. The mixture of emotions that I had when I realized what he had planned must have been obvious.

"If you feel uncomfortable at any time, I promise I will take you back. No pressure."

I followed him towards the lighthouse where tourists could be seen standing outside of the pre-19th-century building. The Italianate-style ivory tower stood behind a sprawling brick keeper's house that now acted as a maritime museum. Purple wildflowers surrounded most of the grounds, except for manicured areas where white and yellow tulips stood tall. As people waited in line to see the inside of the tower, we continued past them through a grove of apple trees, until we came to a small stretch of beach that most people hadn't realized existed.

When we stepped beyond the wildflowers onto the beach, I immediately took off my shoes. As the warm grains filled the spaces between my toes, I looked across the water remembering how beautiful it was there. The lake expanded as far as I could see in every direction, and the breeze tossed the waves softly towards us. The tide was low, so Nick spread a thick blanket across a section of sand close to the shoreline. While he emptied the basket and prepared the space, I walked close enough to the water that waves began to wash over my feet.

I hadn't been there since the night after I graduated from law school. After enduring hours of painful small talk at the dinner party Lola had thrown me for my graduation, Nick and I snuck off by ourselves. I raided Lola's wine cabinet, and we drove around Evanston in hopes of finding a quiet park by the lake. After taking a wrong turn, we saw a bright light beaming through an orchard of trees and decided to keep driving until we figured out what was there. Once we got to the clearing, we were astonished by the sight of the historic tower. Though the building was closed, we opened a bottle of wine and walked around its grounds until we accidentally discovered the hidden beach.

I had a few weeks before I started my bar exam preparation, but Nick was leaving in less than a month to begin his post-doctoral fellowship at the Centre for European Research in Microfinance in Brussels. For months, I tried to prepare myself for when he would leave but the closer we got to his departure, the more difficult it became to imagine what my life would be like without him.

Drinking wine out of the bottle, we sat on the beach and talked for hours until we eventually fell asleep lying in the sand. It wasn't until Lola called my cell phone and woke us up that we realized that it was past midnight.

"She's angry," I said when I got off the phone with her.

"I love you," Nick uttered in his half-awake state.

I wished he hadn't said it, although I already knew that he did. Even though I felt the same way, I hesitated in saying it back.

"And water is wet," I replied, pulling him up off the ground, trying to make light of the moment.

He steadied himself on his legs. "It's okay to say that you love me too," he said sarcastically.

"I know...but saying it makes things more complicated. Besides, it shouldn't matter if I say it or not since you obviously already know that I do."

"It matters to me," he said seriously.

"Why?" I asked as I pulled him into the wooded area back towards our car.

"Because I feel vulnerable now that I said it," he joked. "And because every man needs to feel wanted."

"But I don't think that love is about wanting someone. I think it's about realizing that you need them."

"It's about both," he said from behind me.

I stopped walking and turned to look at him. "So if this is what you need then here it is. I love you, Nick. I love you so much that it scares me. I love you so much that thinking of your happiness makes me smile. I love you so much that the fact that you will be leaving for Brussels in a few weeks makes me sick to my stomach. I love you so much that I'm telling you that I love you even though I swore to myself that I would not say it before you left."

He smirked. "Now was that so difficult?"

"Yes, it was," I lied.

"That just makes it mean that much more to me," he said as he took my hand and led me back to the car.

I didn't realize that Nick was watching me until I turned around. Though I was enjoying the warm water roll across my feet, I went to sit next to him on the blanket. Before I could object, he grabbed a towel from the basket and began to dry my feet.

"I want you to ask me anything that you have always wanted to know about me," he said.

"Why, is there something that you want to tell me?" I asked, feeling put on guard by his request.

We had only been there for a few minutes, but I was already regretting leaving Lola's house. Being back on the beach was a painful reminder of how happy we had once been. If the fate of our relationship rested on us taking a walk down memory lane, then I knew our conversation would go nowhere fast. It wasn't that I had nothing to ask him or was afraid of what he might ask me. I was afraid to know how he really felt about me.

"Indulge me," he demanded, passing me a bottle of water from his bag.

He continued, "I want you to ask me anything that you've always wanted to know, no matter what it is. I just need for you to allow me to do the same. The only stipulation is that we can't lie to each other. If we can't be honest with each other at this point in our relationship, then there is no point to any of this."

"So do you think that you can be as honest as you are asking me to be?" I challenged.

"I do. That's why I brought you out here," he said. "During the past week, I have been thinking about how we got to this place. As much as I wanted to blame it on a single event, the truth is that I've always thought that there's a wall between us. I never knew how to get past it. It was there long before you became pregnant and long before I got the job in Paris."

He cleared his throat. "So here is my question to you. Do you or have you ever blamed me for Layla's death?"

I was speechless. Thoughts of the day she died began to swarm through my head. Though I had never admitted it to anyone, not even Lola, in the early days after Layla's death, I did resent Nick for being the reason that I was late getting to her apartment that day. Rationally, I knew that her death wasn't his fault, but in the hours after she died, I not only blamed him but myself.

"I was angry at you and I did blame you, initially," I admitted. "I resented you the day she died and maybe the entire week afterwards because I needed to be upset at someone. I wished that I was there with her so she wouldn't have felt alone. I did wish that I were with her that day and not with you. You asked me not to lie, so I won't lie to you about that."

He looked out at the water as I spoke. I could see that he wanted to ask me something else, but he was cautious.

"What?" I asked him, already feeling like I had said too much.

"Can I ask you a follow-up question without you becoming upset?"

"Okay," I said hesitantly.

"If you only blamed me initially, why did you wait two weeks before telling me that she died?"

"Because I was trying to deal with it I had checked-out on everyone. I didn't talk to anyone," I said defensively. "And I didn't know how to tell you what happened without it appearing like I blamed you."

He looked as if he was considering the truthfulness of my response. When a few minutes passed without him saying anything, I asked my first question.

"Why didn't you go to Brussels?" I asked.

A week before Nick was set to begin his job at CERMi, he showed up at my house in the middle of the night. When I answered the door, he got down on one knee and teasingly asked me to marry him, though I could tell that he had too many drinks. The following morning I helped him nurse his hangover and he told me that the paperwork for his Brussels' work permit was stalled in mounds of bureaucratic red tape. He explained that since he was unable to report to CERMi by the month's end, that he had to relinquish his position. The details of the story never added up to me, but a week later Nick received an offer to return to the Economics Department as an assistant professor, so I never had the nerve to probe further.

"It was because of you," Nick replied, more matter-of-fact than I anticipated.

Our lives over the past few years started slowly to make sense. If he walked away from his position at the renowned organization, then he compromised his professional reputation before it even began. Word probably spread quickly among the academic community, which explained why he worked so hard to maintain good standing for himself once he was at the University.

"Do you resent me for your decision to stay?" I asked.

"I resented having to give up something I had been working for long before you and I ever met. Yes, at times, I think some of that regret was unfairly directed at you, even though I recognized that if I told you before I made my decision then you would have told me to go. I didn't want you to feel responsible for a choice that I made. I tried to convince myself, for months, that it was okay for me to go, but it never felt right. I asked CERMi if I could report a month later, and they told me no. So I decided to stay."

"Have you stayed with me all this time because you felt guilty about Layla?" I asked him.

For years, I wondered why he decided to stay at the university instead of pursuing other opportunities to work internationally. Deep down, I always feared a sense of obligation, rather than love, explained his never leaving.

"I did feel guilty, but that's not why I stayed," he admitted. "I felt responsible for making you late that day. For a long time I felt like it was my duty to make you sure you were happy and if you weren't, I saw it as my fault. I saw it as my responsibility to try to fix you."

"You thought you had to fix me?" I asked him again, needing clarity.

"I've never doubted the reasons why I love you, even though I knew that you always have. I couldn't ignore that the death of your sister turned the woman I first met into someone who was broken and fragile. Despite how much you would try to hide it from everyone, you remained that way for a very long time. It was presumptuous of me, but I saw it as my role to protect you from anything that could hurt you."

I hated that Nick thought that I was too fragile to take care of myself. In some ways, he was right. A part of me never fully recovered after Layla died. The thought of losing someone else that I loved was so unbearable that I built a wall around myself. Many people had told me that I had grown colder, but the truth that I had forced myself to become numb.

"Is this why you lied about Paris for months?" I asked with a hint of anger in my voice.

"It's my turn," Nick replied, ignoring my question.

He turned his body to look directly at me. From the look in his eyes, I was sure that he had somehow found out about Gabe.

"You asked me two questions. I'm going to ask you two, okay?"

I nodded hesitantly.

"Do you truly want to know what happened that night? And do believe that you could truly forgive me?"

"Yes," I replied to both questions.

"When I left the hospital, I drove around for a long time trying to figure out what I should do. I went home hoping to find you there so I could explain to you why I didn't tell you the truth. After half the day passed without hearing anything from you, I honestly started to wonder if you were ever going to come back. I asked my co-worker to meet me for a drink. She previously taught at the Sorbonne, and I wanted to know whether she thought I could realistically defer without completely losing my fellowship."

He stopped and looked as if he was calculating his words.

"No half-truths, Nick. I want to know what happened," I said.

"You didn't see what you thought that you saw," he said, now looking at me directly in my eyes.

"Nick, if you weren't kissing her then what were you doing, whispering in her ear?"

"Yes, that's exactly what I was doing."

He hesitated for a moment and for the first time his eyes shifted to the ground. "I was completely at fault because I met up with a woman who I knew wanted to sleep with me. I convinced myself that it made sense to call her, but the truth is that I wanted to be with someone who simply wanted to be with me. I didn't want to be with someone I knew resented me or could only tolerate my presence for minutes at a time. That's what our relationship had become. I just wanted to see what it felt like to have a woman look at me and want to be with me," he said looking me directly in my eyes. His voice was quiet but resolute.

I wanted to be upset, but I had no right. He was braver than I was to admit why he was looking for something that he needed from someone else.

"What did you whisper to her?"

He looked embarrassed. "I told her that she reminded me so much of you that I wanted to kiss her. I told her that if I had one more scotch I would have probably tried to sleep with her. Then I told her that I needed to get home to the woman who I promised to love forever, even if she doesn't want to love me back."

I looked into his eyes, and I knew that he was telling the truth. As hurt as I felt, I immediately thought of the kiss that I shared with Gabe, and I became overwhelmed with guilt again. I wanted to tell him everything, but I knew, just as Lola predicted, that admitting it to him would be more about alleviating my guilt than saving our marriage.

Forcing the idea of confessing out of my mind, I asked him the one question that we both had been avoiding.

"Nick, what should we do about Paris?"

He reached into the basket and pulled out an envelope. As soon as I saw its shape, I knew what it was.

"It's an open ticket," he said, holding my hands in his.

"I have to go to Paris. If I don't, I won't resent you but I'll resent myself. I have to leave to secure the rental house at the end of July, but I will be back, no matter what, for the delivery of our child."

I didn't try to hold back my tears. "There's nothing that I can do to convince you to stay, is there?" I asked, as my mind began to spin around the reality that he was leaving.

"I need to do this for me and us. I am committed to you and her," he said, rubbing my stomach. "But I will not be the best father or husband I can be if I give up the one thing that I been working towards my entire career. That's not the man you married."

I looked down at the ticket in my lap. The thought of a commuter marriage seemed as ill-fated as a long-distance college relationship.

"This feels like an ultimatum," I said quietly.

"It's not an ultimatum because I still choose our family regardless of whatever you decide to do. I chose you, and I am willing to figure this out whether we are physically together or apart. I just need to know whether you are still committed to us," he said guardedly, and his eyes searched mine for an answer.

I couldn't help but think that the fact that he was willing to go to Paris alone was proof that he wanted to move on with his life. The most painful revelation was that I was no longer in a position to convince him to stay.

He reached into the picnic basket and pulled out a small cake and two plates. As soon as I saw the hazelnut cake layered with chocolate buttercream, I knew that it came from Bitter Sweet, the bakery that catered our wedding. Never in a million years would I have thought that its name would so adequately come to describe our marriage.

"This is a week late but I never got the chance to say Happy Birthday to you," he said as he placed a single candle in its middle. After he lit it, I closed my eyes and blew out the flame.

"Did you make a wish?" he asked.

"I did," I replied. "It was for you to finally have everything that you have ever wanted."

He leaned over and kissed me. With each touch of his lips, I tried to remember the softness of his mouth. He pulled me closer into his arms and in silence we watched the waves edge closer to our feet as the sun set beyond the lake. Though neither of us would admit it, we both feared that we had just said goodbye.

TWENTY-ONE

"Puna, sit down. There's nothing left to do," my mother said from behind me as she continued to sway on Lola's patio swing.

When I turned to look at her, I realized that even after a year I still wasn't used to seeing her hair cut short. Unlike Lola, Layla and me, her hair was naturally long, straight and jet-black which always made her look more like one of my friends than my mother. As a child, I loved playing with her hair because it looked and felt so different from my own. So when she decided to cut most of it off, days before she and my father moved away, a small part of me mourned it along with her and my father's daily physical presence.

Eden's friends were all gone, and the only reminder of her party was the confetti from her piñata scattered through Lola's yard. Once Lola took Eden into the house for her bath, my mother and I stayed in the yard. We had been cleaning for almost an hour before my mother sat down and poured herself a glass of wine. As a retired academic, she commonly joked that she 'no longer believed in hard work' and would rather spend her days 'doing what she wants, with whom she wants, in the way in which she wants to do it'. By the look of the way that she gazed up at the stars, I knew that cleaning up was no longer very high on her to-do list.

Picking up the last garbage bag filled with paper shreddings, I headed to Lola's driveway to dump it in her trashcan. I was only able to take two steps before my mother called after me again.

"Lotus, I'm serious. Time to sit down and get off your feet."

My mother's tone made me stop in my tracks. Instead of walking the bag to the front of the house, I tied a knot in it and sat it against Lola's patio doors. Knowing there was no point in trying to deny her demands, I took off my shoes and went to sit next to her.

Reaching past her, I picked up her glass of wine and sniffed it.

"I miss wine," I said as I closed my eyes. "This would be the perfect night to take a bottle and go to the lighthouse and fall asleep."

"The lighthouse, huh?" she echoed suspiciously. "That must be where you and Nicholas went during the party."

"It is," I answered, avoiding eye contact with her.

I had been thinking about our conversation all day, and I was still processing the idea of Nick leaving.

I waited for her finally to ask me what was going on between Nick and me but to my surprise, she didn't. After spreading her blanket across my legs, she focused her attention back to the book that was in her hands. I rested my head on her shoulders as we swung in silence, enjoying the breeze that was blowing through Lola's yard.

My eyes began to grow heavy, and I felt myself drifting to sleep. Just as I heard myself beginning to snore, she nudged me.

"Go to bed, Puna. I don't want you to catch a cold staying out here with me."

"No, this is perfect, Mom. I'll stay out here with you until you are ready to go inside," I said after resting my head back on her shoulders.

I closed my eyes again. I knew that I wouldn't fall back to sleep, but I wanted to stay out there with her as long as possible. I felt just as I had as a little girl sitting next to her, safe and momentarily without a care in the world. Just as I felt myself beginning to relax again, she nudged me.

"I've waited a whole week, Lotus. I think it's time for you to start talking," she said.

With my eyes still closed, I contemplated pretending that I asleep. When I felt the swing slowly come to a stop, I knew that I had no choice but to talk.

I opened my eyes, and she was staring at me. I knew if I didn't say anything, an interrogation would surely be on its way. I began to tell her everything that had happened over the past six months, from the day I first saw Gabe in the emergency room of Lakeshore Medical to the conversation Nick and I had that afternoon. I didn't keep any detail from her, not even the fact that I kissed Gabe.

"So that's why you were crying at your wedding?" she asked.

She continued to hold my hand as we both stared out into the darkness that surrounded us. Though she already knew the answer, I couldn't bring myself to say yes or no. I was embarrassed and ashamed to admit that I thought of Gabe throughout that morning up until the moment I walked down the aisle. Since she had been married to my father for almost forty years, I didn't expect my mother to understand. I prepared myself for her judgment.

"Are you completely disgusted with me?" I asked as I looked down at the grass that brushed my bare feet.

"I'm not your judge. I'm your mother, sweetheart. This is your life to figure out, not mine. I love you, and I'm here to help you navigate it, but you are not a little girl. I can't tell you what to do or how you should feel. You are going to have to be the one to separate your desires from your fears, and figure out what to do with them."

"It feels like a typhoon has come through my life," I said, closing my eyes again. "Everything that I thought was certain just a year ago isn't anymore."

"Maybe the need to be 100 percent certain about everything is exactly what's gotten you in trouble."

It was an odd response coming from my mother. Having grown up with her using the Socratic Method on us as children, I knew that she was trying to lead me to asking her the right question rather than revealing it to me herself.

"Do you know anything about Taoism?" she asked.

She glanced in my direction just in time to see me roll my eyes. No one liked talking about religion more than my mother, and there was no way to be sure if our conversation would ever return to anything that had to do with my life.

"Trick question, right?" I asked, leaning my head back on her shoulders.

She smirked and continued to push our swing with her feet. "I know you hate it when I talk about religion, but this might be helpful. Taoists believe in the concept of dualism, as in two opposites making a whole. You've seen the yin and the yang symbol before, right?"

"Of course I have, Mom," I said, secretly hoping that wherever she was headed it wouldn't end with referencing Tom Cruise saying, 'You complete me.'

"Well, the yin and the yang symbolize the opposite forces that lie within every person, and everything in the universe. So if you were to try hard enough, you could probably describe every person on this Earth perfectly with just two words, which would most likely be very different from each other."

"Mom..."

"Just listen," she said. "So Taoists believe that everyone has a dual nature within – an attribute that pushes them to their best self and an attribute that tries to counteracts that. They believe that only when we figure out how to balance the two sides, do we find peace," she said.

"For example, Lola is brave but impulsive, so her courage often gets her into situations over her head. As a result, the recognition of her impulsiveness forces her to moderate when to act courageously and when to be silent."

She paused and smiled. "Layla, on the other hand, was wise beyond her years, but she was also a bit naïve. As smart as she was, she looked at everything in life through rose-colored lenses. That caused her a fair share of hurt feelings and heartache, but it forced her to realize that her intelligence could only reveal to her so much, that there would be some things that, no matter if she read every book in the world, she wouldn't understand."

She paused again, but I knew what she must have been feeling. Even though Layla had been gone for six years, referencing her in the past tense never felt right. Her presence still lingered in our lives. On most days, it felt like she was still here, just away on a very long vacation. I cradled my stomach thinking of how scared I had been just a week before, when I thought I might lose my child whom I had yet to meet. For the first time, I had a fleeting understanding of what my mother may have felt since Layla left us.

She turned her body inward so that my head could fall on her chest. I held my breath, waiting to hear just how dysfunctional my mother thought I was.

"Do you know which two words I would use to describe you?" she asked.

"Should I be scared?"

She laughed. "And there lies your challenge, Lotus. Your words are: extraordinarily determined but painfully insecure."

"Technically that's four words," I said, trying to make light of what she said. "Besides, don't you think that 'painfully insecure' is a bit of an exaggeration?"

"Okay, maybe that was a bit harsh," she said, laughing to herself.

My mother was always the brutally honest parent, which was a stark contrast to my father's quiet and calm demeanor. Her candor led to many arguments between my sisters, her and I during our teenage years though I had come to admire her forthrightness as an adult. Ironically, it wasn't until Layla's death that my mother sought to soften her approach. It was nice to see that now she weighed the impact of her words as equally as the points she wanted to make.

"Maybe 'fear-driven' is a better way to put it. Once you decide that you are going to do something no one can keep you from achieving your goal. That's what got you into the London School of Economics. That's how you managed to push through your last semester of law school after your sister died. For all of your determination, you always seem to doubt whether you deserve the things that you receive from your effort. As a result, I think it's often difficult for you to find contentment, because even when you get what you've worked for – or the things that you want - you convince yourself that you didn't deserve them. The few times that I have seen you accept when good things happen to you, I think you still wait for something to come along and ruin it. Did you have to read Tolstoy while in college?"

My thoughts were back at the lighthouse. My mind began to weave together the things that Nick had said with my mother's opinion of me.

"Puna," my mother said again, jolting my attention back to her.

"Yes, I've read Tolstoy," I said, still bothered by her comments.

"Well, Tolstoy said, 'Happiness is pleasure without the remorse.' You allow yourself pleasures, but you can't let go of the remorse."

"So you think that I am fragile?" I asked casually, thinking of my earlier conversation with Nick.

She moved her shoulder from under my head and forced me to sit up and face her. "Of course I don't think you are weak, Lotus. Sometimes, I just think that you exchanged your backbone for a wishbone, or for a blindfold for that matter," she said, making herself laugh.

Despite what she was saying, it made me happy to see her laughing. She never believed in taking oneself too seriously and forbid wallowing in self-pity for too long. Seeing her mock me made me believe, in a strange way, that I might come out of all of this okay.

"Mom," I said, interrupting her.

"Oh. Sorry, honey. I didn't mean to laugh. I just want you to ask yourself why you can't let go of someone who hurts you, and why you are willing to lose a person who has proven that he loves you. You need to ask yourself why it's easier for you to hold on to love that has already caused you a great amount of pain. I've had many men love me in my life, and each of them said they were willing to give up many things to be with me. But the one who I chose to spend my life with is the one who did."

Her words felt like an indictment. "So you after everything that I told you – including how Nick spent the past six months completely ignoring the fact that I was pregnant, and how he willingly went to a bar to meet up with someone who probably wanted to sleep with him – after all of that, you think that I am an idiot?"

"No, I don't think you are an idiot. I think you are lying to yourself to get what you believe that you want. Nick may have been an ass, but now you know why. Honestly, Lotus, you are too smart to tell me that you didn't know that Nick gave up his fellowship five years ago for you."

She was right. When I turned my face away from her, she held my chin and made me look at her in the eye.

"Sweetheart, I get it and I am not here to judge you or tell you what to do with your life. You didn't ask him because you didn't want to know that he gave up something that meant that much to him for you. If you had to acknowledge what he gave up then you would have to acknowledge that you didn't think that you were worth the sacrifice. But you need to finally accept that you are worth it."

Holding my face in her hands, she wouldn't let me look away. As my eyes filled with tears, I felt both embarrassed and relieved for reasons I couldn't explain.

She lifted her blanket from our laps and wiped my face.

"Like I said, my life feels like a catastrophe," I said, suddenly feeling exhausted.

She wrapped her arms around me. "Sweetie, live long enough and you will learn that catastrophes can be a good thing. They force you to start over and rebuild your life the way that you want, rather than you way you have accepted it to be. Just be prepared, because you will have to love one of these men enough to let him go in the end."

The 3rd Trimester

TWENTY-TWO

"How was your day?" Gabe asked as he walked me through the long hallway leading to his loft. "Did you have an appointment?"

"No, it was yesterday," I replied, trying to change the subject before he could ask the obvious follow-up question. "How are you? You look tired."

"I am tired, but I'm off for the next two days. Did you go to the doctor by yourself?" He tried to inquire casually as he escorted me into his living room.

I couldn't help but pause when I stepped into the room and saw his floor-to-ceiling windows that overlooked downtown and the north branch of the Chicago River. It was one of the best views of the city that I had ever seen.

"Nick went with me," I said before walking to the windows and peering down at the stream of boats sailing through the channel.

He ignored my response so I could tell that he was bothered, but we both knew that he wasn't in a position to take issue with me seeing my husband. Though a month had passed since I was discharged from the hospital, he respected the space that I explained that I needed and resorted to calling to check on me every evening. I declined several invitations from him to meet for dinner until that day, when I stopped by before driving to Lola's house after work.

"Traffic going back to Evanston is horrible right now, so I decided to hang out in the city until rush hour is over. I didn't think that you were at home but since I had a meeting a few blocks away, I decided to take a chance and see," I said as I made myself comfortable on his couch.

"I'm glad that you did," he said with a gentle smile. "I'm happy to see you. Do you want something to drink?"

I agreed, and he disappeared behind a wall for several minutes. Neither of us said anything while he prepared our drinks, though we could have easily continued our discussion. He was waiting for me to initiate the conversation, and I wasn't sure if I had the nerve yet. In his mind I knew there was nothing left for us to talk about other than what I had decided to do about *us*.

While he was still hidden behind the kitchen walls, I looked around his loft for signs of his fiancée but saw nothing. There were only abstract paintings and massive bookshelves wrapped around the entirety of his place. They were adorned with medical books and wooden tribal masks from his various trips around the world. There was a sterility about his home that made it impossible to tell whether he had removed all remnants of her before I had arrived, or whether there was never any sign of her presence in his home in the first place. I wanted to know about their relationship, but I refused to ask. A part of me felt guilty, but I assumed that he wanted me to know as little about his fiancée as I wanted him to know about Nick.

"I need to ask you something," I said once he finally returned to the room with two cups of tea.

He sat down on the couch across from me. "I assumed as much," he after taking his first sip.

He was nervous though he tried his best not to show it. My hands grew clammy as I searched for the courage to say what I wanted to say.

"Just ask me," he said, seeing my hands begin to fidget.

I smiled nervously in response. I cleared my throat and took a long deep breath inward.

"Why didn't you call me after Layla died?" I blurted out. "Not just after she died, but in the weeks and years afterward? After everything you said in the hospital that day, why did you disappear?"

"I didn't."

"You did, Gabe. Even as we made plans to bury Layla, I waited for you to call but you never did. You obviously made a decision to stay as far away from me as possible, and I never understood why. If you always loved me as much as you say, why did you vanish?"

I saw a combination of sadness and regret in his eyes. His lack of a response made it apparent that he didn't anticipate me asking him that question, though it was the one thing that had haunted me most about him for years.

"Where is this coming from?" he asked.

"Are you surprised that, after all this time, this is what I need to know? You didn't think that I would need to understand how you could decide to tell me after five years that you still loved me but in the next breath, disappear? Don't you think that after everything that happened ten years ago — when I got on a plane to find you cheating on me — that I would need to know why your words always contradict your actions? You want me to risk everything, to take you at your word that you will be there, but our past has demonstrated just the opposite."

He continued to stare straight ahead into the maze of buildings that surrounded us, looking as if he was calculating what he wanted to say.

"Why are you *really* asking me this, Lotus?" he asked, finally breaking his silence.

"Because I need to know."

"No, that's a lie because you already know. I told you that I loved you the day Layla died because I did, and I still love you more than I am capable of loving anyone else," he said.

"What I told you before is the truth. I didn't reach out to you because I was afraid of hurting you. I was scared that I wouldn't be able to give you whatever it was that you needed during that time. My past mistakes made me believe that you deserved better than me. I didn't think that you..."

"But I did need you," I said, finishing his thought.

"I will always regret not being there for you. I was stupid and afraid. But as a man who knows himself better than I did back then, I know that there is no one who can love you more than I do right now, and that's all that matters to me. I want you even though I know there is a chance that I can't have you. But until you tell me that I can't, until you tell me that you don't love me, you can't convince me to stop trying."

Though the setting sun continued to shine brightly through his windows, suddenly the room felt cold. Neither of us spoke as the room began to grow darker, and the city below us seemed to stand still. Our past felt like an uninvited guest in the room, and I started to believe that its presence would always be standing between us.

"You still don't know, do you?" he asked as the last hint of natural light disappeared from the room.

"Know what?" I asked.

"You still don't know what you want. So this is you deciding to settle for what you have," he said without looking at me. "It's easier to convince yourself that I can't love you as much as your husband, rather than to accept the fact that you know that I can. You want to try to convince me of my feelings and tell me that my mistakes mean that I can't love you. If this is what you need to do to keep yourself from making the decision that you want to make, then you can save both of us the agony and just go home to your husband."

"I didn't come over here to argue with you," I said as I began to gather my things to leave.

"Then what do you want?" he yelled.

"This isn't about me, Gabriel."

"This conversation is as much about you as it is about me," he challenged. "Lotus, tell me what you want."

"You are turning this around on me, but I asked YOU a direct question about YOUR actions, not mine. Don't turn this around on me because you don't want to answer it."

"Dammit, Lotus, stop thinking that I am trying to manipulate you. I just want to know. What do you want? Why is it so hard for you to say what you want?" he asked.

"I want to not be scared anymore," I yelled back at him so loudly that my voice was shaking.

As soon as the words left my mouth I felt like something that I had hidden from everyone had just become visible for him to see.

"I want to know that I won't lose another person I love. I want to know that the person who says that he will love me until I die will be there like he promised. I want to know that you will always be there for me. I want to be able to give you every flawed piece of me and believe that it's good enough. I want to know that my child will be loved. I want to not be afraid of you leaving me again."

He walked over to me and time stood still. As pulled me into his arms, we were back in his college apartment, two kids who were afraid to accept their feelings for each other. We stood there for what felt like eternity, content that for the first time, nothing else had to be said.

"I swear I will never let go of you again," he whispered in my ear.

We stood in the middle of his condo, swaying back and forth to a song that would be inaudible to anyone but us.

"I've missed you so much," he whispered as he kissed my forehead. "All this time, all these years, I wondered if you were okay. I needed you to be okay. I even tried shopping in your parent's old neighborhood for a while, hoping to see you, but I never did. I just wanted a chance to see you again."

I wanted to tell him so much of what had happened in my life over the past few years, but I decided none of that mattered. I just didn't want the moment to pass. When the sun finally set, the only thing that lit the room where we lay together on his couch was the glow of the illuminated skyline. Though we were fully clothed, each kiss that he placed on my forehead felt more intimate than the next.

"Promise me that whatever you decide, it won't be based on something that I did in the past," he said.

"I promise you that I will not make a decision based on our past," I whispered back to him before falling asleep in his arms.

TWENTY-THREE

"I think you should tell her," I heard Dakota whisper to Lola as I walked down the stairs.

"Tell me what?" I said once I stopped to put on my heels at the bottom of the stairway. "Please don't tell me that you are knocked up again. Two pregnant women in one family are more than either of us can tolerate."

She glanced over at Dakota and smiled back at me endearingly.

"No, idiot. I just wanted to tell you that you look beautiful tonight."

"I know that you are lying, but I'll take any compliment that I can get at this point. I already feel like the ugly stepsister walking in there with the two of you tonight," I joked as Lola and Dakota followed me into the living room, holding their champagne glasses in one hand and their heels in the other.

"Seriously, I appreciate you all for coming with me to the ball. Even though it will be work for me, I promise that it will be a good time for both of you."

"I don't know how you can have two men and one baby daddy but still manage to have no date to this damn thing," Dakota quipped as she found a seat on Lola's couch and began to put on her stilettos.

"Nick leaves tomorrow and there was no way I could invite Gabe. I figured that this could be our final girl's night out. It will be like our private celebration to usher in the beginning of my third trimester, and the end of life as I now know it. So drink up, ladies, get ready for a good time and eat all the seafood and caviar you can get your hands on," I said as I raised my glass of sparkling cider in the air and led them to the limo that was waiting for us in Lola's driveway.

As soon as we arrived at the Drake Hotel, I saw Elizabeth standing across the street under a lit gazebo, on her phone. Once we got out of the car, she motioned for me to come over, so I directed Lola and Dakota into the main lobby where I could already hear the bands beginning to warm up. After several minutes of overhearing her angle for a last-minute donation, she finally hung up and turned to me with a smile.

"Lotus, you look absolutely stunning, my dear. I see you wore the dress that I sent over. I knew that a J. Mendel dress would perfectly hide that big belly of yours," she said as she grabbed my hand and led me across the street, inside of the famed hotel.

I wanted to tell her that I wasn't necessarily interested in hiding my stomach, but I didn't want to risk offending her.

"Elizabeth, thank you again. I had no idea what I was going to wear."

"It was the least I could do for all of your hard work on this event, and besides, it's especially important for you to look the part tonight. As you know, this is an important night, not only for the Foundation, but for you. I want people to begin to see you in a position of authority moving forward."

Though Elizabeth was aware of Nick's fellowship in France, she made it no secret that she assumed that I was going to stay.

"Did you bring the checkbook?" she asked.

I nodded as we entered through the doors of the legendary building. Though all the vendors had been paid beforehand, I found it odd that she called me that morning and asked me to bring my set of business checks to the ball. I was about to ask her whether there were any outstanding expenses that I overlooked when the sight of the ballroom left me speechless.

"I know, honey. That was my reaction as well. It is beyond marvelous," she said, reading my mind.

In the past, the event was in a larger venue to accommodate public donors. This year the board opted for the more private and classic venue of the post-Renaissance hotel. Gold, black and white balloons filled the ceiling just above the crystal chandeliers and Chiavari chairs wrapped in silk encircled each of the tables set with massive red rose centerpieces. Trees adorned with tea lights outlined the room, creating an illusion of a winter paradise though it was the middle of summer.

"This is absolutely breathtaking. I can't believe that it all came together," I thought aloud.

As the band began to play, I turned my attention to looking for my sister and cousin.

Elizabeth read my mind. "Go have fun and enjoy the night. We both deserve it. The hard part is over but do not disappear because I'll need you at the end of the night."

When I finally found Dakota and Lola, they were on the dance floor doing their best versions of the foxtrot with two wealthy donors whose faces I recognized from a Chicago business magazine. As I watched them add shimmies and swinging hair to the traditionally stiff dance, I laughed harder than I had in a long time. For a fleeting moment, I imagined the possibility of my life in Paris without them. They had always been there to see me through the most difficult times of my life. They knew my insides, my most genuine joys, most painful moments, and every experience that happened in between. The times when I felt so lost they were always there to be my compass. It was difficult to imagine any moments to come, whether happy or sad, without them close by my side. Pushing the sad thoughts from my mind, I decided to focus on taking in the moment – not only because of what it had taken to get here but because I also recognized that soon things would never be the same.

After dancing nonstop through three more songs, Lola and Dakota finally made it over to our table. Over the course of the next four hours, we ate and laughed more than we had in years. After an 80-year-old, married bank executive propositioned Dakota for sex; I couldn't envision how the evening could get any better. It wasn't until the band played Nick's and my wedding song that I thought about the following day and what it meant for our marriage.

Dakota caught me looking down at my watch and somehow knew exactly what I was thinking. "I think we should leave here early and have the limo drop you off at your house so you can have a goodbye booty call with your husband," she said with a mischievous grin.

"Probably not a good idea," I laughed. "I offered to take him to the airport, but he insisted on taking a cab since his flight is so early in the morning. So technically I said 'goodbye' to him before I got dressed for the gala. Honestly, I think the only way I am getting through the night is because I'm in a state of denial. I keep trying to figure out if our marriage is already over but we both are just too scared to say the words."

"Do you have any regrets?" Dakota asked.

"I suspect that I will have a thousand regrets the second he gets on the plane," I admitted.

Elizabeth appeared behind me and tapped me on my shoulder. "Lotus, we need you at the corporate donors' table. Will you both excuse her for a moment? And don't forget to bring your dossier."

When we arrived at the head table, Elizabeth escorted me to a seat between her and the director, who was laughing louder and more obnoxiously than usual. His inebriation became apparent when, after untying his silk bow tie, he kissed me on the cheek and insisted on introducing me to the entire table.

"Ladies and gentlemen, please let me introduce you to our managing director of operations. She's a ballbuster, but she is the smartest person that I've worked with in a very long time. I know that I'm not supposed to announce this yet, but she will be the new executive director of the Foundation at the end of the year after she pops out this baby and gets her figure back."

Though I should have foreseen it, the announcement shocked me as much as the standing round of applause that followed. My mind was still spinning as I took the seat next to him and listened to Elizabeth speak proudly to the donors in the room about the Foundation's work and her dreams for its legacy. I was still digesting the news when she returned to the table and quietly asked the Director and me to meet her in the hallway.

Elizabeth led us to a private seating area on the other side of the lobby. As soon as we sat down, she turned to me and asked me again if I had brought the Foundation's checkbook.

She handed me a pen from out of her purse, "Now, we just need for you to write a check from the Foundation in the amount of $750,000."

The request and the amount startled me. It was nearly everything we had fundraised from the night, and she knew that in order to write a check for that amount, I needed the board's approval.

She handed me the name of an organization I didn't recognize on a piece of paper. "You can make the check out to this company."

The uneasiness that I felt was painfully familiar. Even if the board would later accept my actions, what she was asking me was legally unethical at best. Looking down at the checkbook in my hand, I knew that if I signed it, I would be permanently aligned not only with Elizabeth but with the director as well. My mind tried quickly to think through what was taking place, but I could hear Nick's voice in my head warning me not to trust Elizabeth.

"I'm sorry, Liz, but I don't feel comfortable doing that without prior board approval," I said, handing the checkbook over to her. "I don't recall the board approving any expenditure for this company, but I'm sure this is something that we can clear up next week with a quick board call."

"When are you going to learn to shut up and do what you are told?" The director yelled loudly at me, dropping his glass of scotch on the floor. "You know that this is for my campaign so just write the damn check so we can all move on."

Seeing me flinch at his outburst, Elizabeth stood between me and director. Though people streaming out of the ball began to look in our direction, she continued to speak softly.

"Lotus, you are the only one other than the executive director who can write checks for the Foundation, so I need you to do this. You should think of this as an opportunity to create your fate. From this point on, I can guarantee that no door will be closed to you professionally. You will not have to worry about how you are going to support yourself or your child. You will be professionally secure for the rest of your life."

I thought again about Nick leaving. Every fear that I had entertained over the last months materialized in my mind. Standing in front of her and the director, I knew that there was no one there to protect me but myself.

"Elizabeth, I'm sorry, but I can't," I said, knowing as I spoke those words that I was also dissolving our relationship.

Before I could say anything else, the executive director cursed and walked away, back towards the ballroom.

"It's fine," Elizabeth said, emotionless as she straightened the creases out of her dress. "I'm sorry for putting you in the position. I see that you are still a starry-eyed girl who thinks that what you want in life should come in a neatly gift-wrapped box. Unfortunately, you fail to understand that no one gets what they want without sacrificing something. I thought you were ready for this, Lotus, but you obviously don't belong at the grownups table yet."

Hearing her words were as painful as seeing the disappointed expression on her face.

She picked up her martini glass and looked at me with cold pity. "Lotus, never forget that what you want is frequently at odds with what most will perceive as being right. You have to choose whether you want to be a content saint or a blissful sinner."

She was shocked when I stepped forward to hug her.

"Thank you for everything, Elizabeth. You are right, I don't belong here and I don't have a desire to play this game. It has been an honor to know and to work for you, but you don't have to wait until Monday to fire me because I quit."

TWENTY-FOUR

When the limo pulled up to the large grey building, I sat in the backseat for a while before I got the nerve to get out of the car. I felt like I had been holding my breath since we left the hotel, but I recognized that I needed to be calm before I went inside. Closing my eyes, I prayed that I wasn't making the biggest mistake of my life. Looking across the seat at Dakota and Lola's concerned stares, I smiled to let them know that I was okay. After I pushed the sickening feeling in my stomach away, I mustered as much courage as I could before opening the door to walk inside.

After waiting in the lobby for ten minutes, he walked through the same double doors where we first re-encountered each other seven months earlier. Though he looked exhausted and tired, I began to take in every inch of his face and write it to my memory. I followed the lines around his long chiseled cheeks and imagined kissing each one of the laugh lines that rested on the sides of his lips. I tried to memorize the exact hue of his dark gray eyes and the thickness of his eyebrows, which had a permanent slight arch downward. I looked at his close-shaven head, and the beard that was beginning to grow along his face. I was grateful that at least this time I could prepare myself to say goodbye, though my effort to do so didn't feel less painful.

"What are you doing here? I got a page saying that you were here. Are you okay?" he asked.

"I am," I replied, pulling him away from the Jamaican security guard who was trying her best to eavesdrop. "Do you have a few minutes to talk?"

He hesitated. "Sure, I guess I can take my break a little early. Do you want to go to one of the sitting rooms in the back?"

"No, we can stay out here."

He scanned my face suspiciously, and I knew he was looking for a telling sign of why I was there. Uninterested in masking how I felt, I took his hand and led him to a set of chairs by the row of vending machines lining the back wall. Somewhere between where we stood and the chairs, he pieced together why I was there. Before I could sit down, he whispered, "Lotus, don't do this."

"Gabe, I know that you love me, but we both know that love isn't enough."

For as long as I could remember, I resented myself every time I cried. Tears felt like unwelcome reminders of how defenseless I secretly always felt; they exposed how afraid I always was. When he held my hand, I didn't try to hold anything back. Afraid of what it would feel like to let go, I let my tears fall until they stained the organza ruffles that covered my legs.

"I can't let you go again," Gabe said, gripping my hand more tightly.

"You don't have a choice," I told him though I was still trying to convince myself that the decision that I was making was the right one.

When he looked at me, I knew that I didn't have to speak the words. He could see that there was nothing that he could say to change my mind.

"Are you still engaged to Ashley?" I asked him.

He immediately grew defensive. "That's not fair, Lotus. Unless I've missed something, you are still married to Nick."

"It's not fair, but I have a right to ask. I promised you that I wouldn't make a decision based on our past, but if your fiancée loves you as much as I once did then I'm no better than the girl who you cheated on me with."

He leaned back and rested his head on the back of his chair. As he stared at the ceiling above him, I stood up to leave.

"I regret what I did to you and I take responsibility for it. But I think it's a cop-out to make this decision based on something that I did when I was twenty-two after my parents divorced."

Looking down at him, I remembered the night in the library when I first realized that I was in love with him.

"You say that you aren't the same person, but you reacted to the same situation in the same exact way. You are committed to someone and rather than be honest with her, the way that I wish you were honest with me, you are allowing her to believe that you are still devoted to her. As someone who knows what it feels like to love you more than anything else, I can't be the one responsible for her living a lie, even if she doesn't realize it."

He let go of my hand, and I knew I would never feel it again. "You are a hypocrite."

"You are right. I may be a hypocrite, but that doesn't make what either of us has done any less screwed up. After everything that we've been through, we should be willing to risk everything for each other, but obviously neither of us willing to do that. We both deserve to be with people who love us enough to risk everything for us. I've just been too dumb to realize that I married that person."

He continued to stare at the ceiling above him. "I lived the last ten years regretting the decision to let you go. I'm not willing to live another decade forcing myself to believe that we aren't supposed to be together."

I looked inside my clutch purse and handed him a letter I had written minutes earlier, in the lobby of the Drake.

"Please read it after I leave. I'm not judging you by the past. I'm judging both of us by the fear that continues to drive the way we make decisions in the present."

He clutched the letter so tightly in his hand I suspected that he was going to ball it up and throw it away. I wanted to ask him to promise me that he would read it, but I decided to respect whatever choice he made.

His beeper began to buzz. From the expression on his face, I knew that he had to leave. As he stood up, he didn't look at me, he just continued to stare at the letter in his hand.

"Lotus, we fell in love when we were too young to be able to handle what that meant. I believe that we do belong to each other. I know that you are my only chance for real happiness. I think you are the one who is terrified, and you are letting that fear make your decisions. But deep down, despite everything you are saying, you know that there is nothing that I wouldn't do for you."

Despite the stares from people around us, I kissed him. When I felt his lips separate from mine, a part of me wished that I could go back in time and do so many things differently.

"People do belong to each other, but I belong to Nick. I'm not willing to sacrifice what I know that I need for what I think that I want. This is me finally freeing myself from the idea that you were the only one who could ever have my heart. I do love you and I will always will, but I now understand that you came back into my life so I could finally let you go."

TWENTY-FIVE

"Are you sure about this?" Lola asked, as she bit her nails in the front seat.

I nodded.

"And you are certain that they will let you fly? Are you sure there is room on the flight? Is it safe to fly this long?" Dakota asked in her typical spit-rapid fashion from the passenger seat.

"Yes. Yes and yes," I said as I changed my clothes in her back seat.

"Don't worry, everything will be fine," Lola said to no one in particular. It was her best attempt to calm each of us, but most importantly herself. I didn't know how she was driving so fast because she hadn't taken her eyes off of my reflection in her rearview mirror.

"Lotus, forget everything that I've said to you up until this point. Just promise me again that you are sure about what you are about to do. I need you to swear that you are positively sure about this. Then I will believe you."

"I'm sure," I said, giving her the most reassuring smile that I could muster from the back seat and with no sleep. "This is the one thing that I am sure about."

I handed Dakota my house keys. "Don't forget that one of you will have to go to my house this week because the movers are coming to get Nick's things. Most of the clothes that I can still fit into are at Lola's house, so just box them and add them to everything else. I'll figure out everything else later."

"We will take care of it, don't worry," Dakota said as she took the keys and stuffed them in her purse.

One after another, they asked me every question that they could think of. As we drove down the interstate to O'Hare International Airport, we went over every contingency plan possible to make sure that I didn't end up stranded in Paris' Charles de Gaulle airport.

"Check again and make sure that you have your passport," Lola demanded.

"And remember to use only your American Express if you have an emergency," Dakota added. "They don't have any foreign transaction fees and they will even increase your balance if you tell them you are stranded overseas."

After checking to make sure that I had packed my prenatal vitamins and an extra pair of compression stockings, they made me recite every detail of my plan again. The excitement that they had an hour before had dissipated, and the gravity of what was happening seemed to hit them at once. As we turned into the terminal, they looked more anxious than I felt, which made me begin to second-guess what I was about to do.

Lola's fingers continued to drum on her steering wheel as we pulled in front of the airline's outdoor check-in station.

Once the car was parked, Dakota turned the radio off and looked back at me. I could see my older sister's eyes still staring at me through the rearview mirror. Just as she looked down, Dakota began to cry.

"Stop it," I said, wiping the tears that were collecting in my own eyes. "I'm tired of crying. Once I get on this plane, I need to know that you all are okay. I can't fly nine hours worried that you all are worried about me. I need to know that even though I am there that nothing will change. When I step on the plane, I need to know that your lives will be great, and that my life will be great, and that this is the best decision I could have made."

It was the most emotional that I had seen Lola in a very long time. Every time she tried to speak, she would cry. I grabbed her hand and kissed it, before opening her door to get my bags out of her trunk.

As one of the skycap assistants greeted me with a luggage carrier, they both got out of the car. Still crying, Lola kneeled down to rub my belly before hugging me.

"I love Nick, but I swear if you are unhappy, I don't want you to think twice about coming home. I will come get you and that baby if I need to. Please don't hesitate to call me collect whenever you need to talk."

I took the book and the envelope she was holding in her hands and placed them in my purse. "I'll be okay, Lola, I promise. I won't be gone forever."

"The flight leaves in an hour, so you are going to have to haul ass to get through security and to the international terminal. Hopefully, you will be able to get some pregnancy pity to get you through the lines faster. Maybe if you wobble a little more, one of those go-carts will take you directly to your gate," Dakota joked through her tears. "Are you sure that you won't have any issues flying? Are you sure that Dr. Solomon said this is okay? Will my little cousin even be an American if she is accidently born in Paris?"

"Dakota, you have got to relax. Your anxiety attack is going to give me an anxiety attack. If Angelina Jolie can fly a plane when she was eleven months pregnant, then I should be able to fly first-class a few days into my third trimester. Dr. Solomon sent my records over to Pitié-Salpêtrière Hospital in Paris a month ago as a precaution. Everything is going to be okay. I promise that I will try my best not to go into labor on the plane," I said as I held my stomach.

The young man who loaded my bags onto a luggage cart coughed to get my attention.

"Your bags will be at the counter, miss," he said before disappearing behind the three of us.

Once he walked away, we stood in a circle on the sidewalk, embracing each other. I wasn't ready to let go of them, but an airport security officer began to yell at Lola to move her truck.

"Amor est aeterna," Lola whispered in my ear.

"Amor est aeterna," I whispered back. "Don't forget to keep your phone close to you."

I had begun to walk towards the check-in counter when Lola called after me. I turned to see her running towards me, despite the airport security officer standing next to her truck writing a parking ticket.

"Lotus, promise me that this is what you want," she said with a hint of angst in her voice.

"This is what I want. You were the one who always told me that the past doesn't matter. The only thing that matters is today, right?" I asked before giving her a final kiss on the cheek and walking through the door.

***

"Oh, sweetie, look at you. You are brave to be flying alone," an older woman said as she checked my passport, ticket, and identification at the security gate.

"My granddaughter's best friend went into labor on the side of the Eisenhower Expressway just last year when she was only 32 weeks. Babies tend to be on their programs and rarely come according to our schedules," she said before handing me back my travel documents.

She had no idea how applicable her words were to my life. "I'm not flying alone. I'm meeting my husband at the gate. We are moving to France," I offered, though her attention was already on the next family in line after me.

Looking at my watch I realized that I had only forty-five minutes to make it through the remainder of the huge labyrinth of the international terminal. Hoping that Nick wouldn't be difficult to find, I rehearsed everything that I wanted to tell him as I walked as fast as I could across the airport.

I finally arrived at the departure gate and could see Nick sitting alone in the distance. Despite the book that he was holding below his face, it was obvious from where I stood that he wasn't reading it. His mind was somewhere else, and I hoped that he was thinking of me.

He glanced up from his book and casually scanned the concourse when our eyes met. I could see the mixture of disbelief and confusion in his eyes as I walked across the concourse to meet him at his seat.

"What are you doing here?" he asked, standing to give me a hug.

"I'm here because I am choosing you like you have always chosen me. You said that you don't want to give up on us but you are about to get on a plane to go to Paris, and I'm in Chicago. That's not fighting for each other. That's running from each other. So I'm here because I choose us, and that means you don't get to go to Paris alone."

I expected him to be happy but his expression remained stoic. He searched my eyes for something that I tried my best to keep hidden from him up until this moment. I knew what he was thinking and waited for him to ask me the obvious.

"What made you change your mind?" he asked. "Don't misunderstand me, I'm happy to see you, and I want nothing more than for you to come with me. But yesterday you seemed sure about your decision; I'm just trying to understand what changed."

Weighing what I wanted against what I knew he deserved, I reached into my purse and pulled out a letter that I had written hours before. Forcing Lola and Dakota's voices out of my head, I placed it in his hand.

"You were able to love me when I was broken, but I don't need to be fixed. I don't need you to save me from myself. I need to know that you can love me despite myself, even despite the things that I have done that may hurt you," I said, sitting in the chair next to him.

"I never asked you to be anyone but yourself."

"You never asked, but exceeding your silent standards became your expectation of me. If I take this leap with you, I need you to accept me for me, even when I fall short because I will. I need you to accept that I am the sum of many things. Things that have been beautiful, painful, great and tragic. I've made many mistakes but you need to be the one who decides whether you can love me, and forgive me, knowing all of that."

"I already love you knowing all of that."

"But you don't know everything," I replied.

He looked down at the envelope in his hands and back at me uneasily. An airline attendant's voice came over the intercom and announced that boarding would begin in five minutes.

"Did you come all this way just to drop this off?" he asked.

"I didn't come just to drop it off but to make sure that you read it before you got on the plane."

He continued to stare at the envelope. I could see the wheels turning in his mind and his hesitancy in asking about its contents. "What would happen if I didn't open this?"

"I would go to Paris with you," I said. "But as much as I wish I could hide everything in that letter from you, I don't want to keep anything from you anymore. I don't want to make a new start with you based off of half-truths or a façade that is more comfortable to believe. I want to go, but ultimately this should be a decision that we make once you know everything you deserve to know."

He looked at me cautiously before he began to peel open the envelope. When he saw the Drake Hotel letterhead on the top of the paper, I interjected, knowing that there was no time to talk about the gala.

"Don't ask," I uncomfortably joked.

He grinned as he slowly began to scan the letter. It wouldn't take long for him to reach my admission about Gabe, and my entire body grew tense as I awaited his response. I forced myself not to look away as he read because if I did, I knew I would never be able to look at him in the eye again. Even if he chose never to forgive me for what I had done, I decided before I wrote the letter that I would forgive myself, because living with guilt was something I no longer had an interest in doing.

A women's voice could be heard announcing that boarding was about to begin. I didn't notice that Nick had finished reading until he stood from his chair with his bags and began to walk towards the area where a line was beginning to form.

I called his name, but he didn't respond.

"Nick," I called after him again.

He finally stopped walking, but he didn't turn around.

"The doctor in the emergency room?" he asked with his back still to me.

"Yes, that was Gabriel," I responded, hearing a tremor in my voice.

He finally turned to me, and his face was unable to mask his anger. Seeing the disappointment in his eyes felt worse than anything that he may have wanted to say.

He didn't respond. Instead, he turned around and continued to walk towards the door leading to the jetway. I was too afraid to follow because I recognized that he had every right to hate me. Paralyzed, I watched him exchange words with the flight attendant who was collecting tickets. I prepared myself to see him disappear behind the partition's doors when he stepped out of line and walked back towards me.

"We have twenty minutes," he said as he grabbed my arm and led me to a row of chairs facing the runways.

Once we sat down, I could see the hurt in his eyes.

"Why did you come here?" he asked me.

"Because I don't want to be without you," I said.

"You mean you are afraid to be without me?"

"No," I corrected him, ignoring the spite in his voice. "I want to be with you because you love me the way that I wish that I could love. I kept asking you to give me more of yourself, but you had already given more than I ever would have dared to ask for. You have been there for me when I needed you the most. That means more to me than anything else."

"If that meant so much, why wasn't that enough?" he asked.

I didn't have an answer to his question that was good enough to tell him. Seeing that the gate area was almost empty, I reached for his hand and was surprised when he let me hold it. A decision was already made and we both knew it. Neither of us spoke as we watched the plane continue to fill with passengers.

"I want to tell you to get on the plane with me. You can't imagine how many times I thought of what it would be like to experience this moment with you. But even if I could forgive you for everything, I'm just tired, Lotus," he said, stopping short.

I wasn't sure if I wanted him to finish his thought, but I asked him anyway. "Tired of what?"

He hesitated, "I'm tired of trying to figure out who I have to be in order for you to trust me. No matter how much I've tried to convince you to believe that I am committed to you all these years, you have always looked for any reason to prove otherwise. I'm tired of trying to convince you that you deserve to be loved."

"You don't have to convince me anymore."

"I *can't* convince you of that anymore," he corrected me.

An announcement was made for the last boarding group. Nick leaned over towards my stomach and kissed it.

"You and her are everything that I never knew that I needed," he said. "I wish I could have been that for you. For what it's worth, I always thought you were more perfect than I deserved. I'm just sorry that I never told you so."

He kissed my forehead. I wanted to cry, but I had no more tears to give. I wanted to tell him that I was willing to do anything to save our marriage, but I suspected that it was already too late.

The flight attendant who had been at the door of the jetway walked over to us. "I'm sorry to interrupt, but the doors to the aircraft will be closing in five minutes," she said.

When she walked away, we hugged.

"You loved me when I was in the darkest place of my life. You wouldn't let go of me when I could barely hold on to myself. How do you expect me to let you go?" I said as I tightened my arms around his shoulders.

"Because neither of us will be able to get what we want unless you do," he said as he softly kissed me on the cheek.

I walked him to the door of the airplane. When he stepped across the threshold, he turned to look back at me. "I'll see you in a month. I love you," he said.

"I love you too, Nick," I whispered as he disappeared beyond the door.

The emptiness that I immediately felt once he was gone was like an unwanted companion. It carried its own physical presence as I stood in front of the large airport windows looking out at the runway. It settled over me like a heavy cloud, until the moment I watched Nick's plane take off in front of me.

***

New groups of people slowly began to stream into the gate area, as if Nick's presence there had only been an illusion. I hadn't moved, but remained motionless in the row of seats that we had shared. I brushed my hand over the seat next to me and could feel that it was still warm. Trying to understand what Nick's absence would mean for my life, I pulled the journal my mother had given me before she left out of my purse. On its cover was an embroidered white lotus flower, etched on a backdrop of black silk. Below it was a Buddhist quote that my mother had told me many times throughout my life.

> *You can search throughout the entire universe for someone who is more deserving of your love and affection than yourself, and that person is not to be found anywhere. You, as much as anybody in the entire universe, deserve your love and affection.*

Unexpectedly I felt the urge to smile, wondering if the Sunday school class that my mother taught knew of her secret Buddhist leanings. When I untied the ribbon that kept it closed, I was surprised to see a handwritten message that she had left for me.

Lotus,

My hope, as you turn the page to begin the next chapter of your own book, is that you let go of the things that have hindered you and believe in the beautiful things that have yet to come. By doing so, you will find is that love tends to flow endlessly to those who make room enough to receive it.

Don't beat yourself up over your mistakes; they will always be the best teachers in showing you who you are. Your daughter will one day

thank you for teaching her that the purest expression of love isn't found in someone else but in having the courage to discover the most authentic version of herself.

Love you and see you soon,

Mom

I wondered if she foresaw how all of this would end. I wondered if she suspected that I would end up alone, in an airport, with a husband and two garment bags on their way to Paris. If she suspected that this was how things would turn out, I wondered why she didn't forewarn me. Perhaps, she believed that this was the best outcome for everyone. I couldn't be sure, but somehow I knew that she would say that things were happening exactly the way that they should.

TWENTY-SIX

A young couple sat down next to me, and I could tell from the woman's fresh French-tip manicure and the way that they wouldn't let go of each other's hands that they were newlyweds. Thinking back to the day of my own wedding, I wondered how a day that was supposed to represent a new beginning could cause a domino effect that forced my present to collide with the past I tried my best to forget.

I felt excruciatingly alone, and it didn't seem fair. I wanted to blame someone, to be angry with Nick or Gabe, but I was alone because of decisions that I had made. Searching my mind for one small thing I should have done differently, so much of what happened still felt beyond my control.

I would never have chosen to see Gabe again, but I couldn't bring myself to regret that I had. Without seeing him, I would have never understood how, in some ways, he, Nick, and I remained stuck in the day that Layla had died. None of us could have realized how that one day would set our lives on the paths that it did. I would have never understood how each of us needed to forgive ourselves for the decisions that we made. Despite everything it cost us, we deserved the closure that each of us spent a decade trying to convince ourselves that we could live without.

Pushing back my tears, I thought about Nick again. I knew that I would love him for the rest of my life. Neither of us could have known at the time, but the vows that we took were simply a hope, an outwardly admission, of what we wanted to believe that we could be. Even if we fell short of forever, because of our daughter I would never doubt that our love was worth every try. I didn't know what the future would bring for us, but I trusted that he would be a great father, even from Paris.

The scene around me grew louder as more people filled the waiting area. I wished for silence, a place where I could hear my thoughts, but I was afraid to move from my chair. If I moved, then I would be forced to figure out what was supposed to come next, and I wasn't prepared for that.

I thought about Layla and how she predicted that I would see Gabe again. I closed my eyes to shut out the busyness around me, and flashes of the dream that I had the morning of my wedding involuntarily began to run through my mind like a silent movie. Gabe and I were back in his college apartment, and again it was the night before our final exams. We stood together in the doorway of his room and just as he did a decade before, he seemed so close that even in my dream I could sense the warmth of his body. Just as we had in real life, I stood nervously holding on to the glass of water he had just given me. Instead of confessing his feelings for me, he gently kissed me and said, "If I knew how much I would have hurt you, I would never have asked you to stay."

In the dream, future memories of what our life could have been together raced through my mind. Instead of lying with me in his bed as he did that evening, he went to the door of his room and stepped on the other side of its threshold. Before closing it, he looked back at me and asked, "I just want to know if you are happy?"

Before I could respond, I woke up.

I opened my eyes to see that the boarding area was almost filled with people again. As I looked over to the couple that was still holding hands next to me, I envied the happiness in their eyes. I knew that I shouldn't feel this way, but I envied that today was the first day of the rest of their lives.

"I never thought I would find someone who could love me as much as you," I heard the woman whisper into her new husband's ear.

I resisted the urge to tell them that love was the easy part, but deciding what they were willing to give up for love was where things usually got tricky. I wanted to tell them that their love could be over as quickly as it began if they weren't willing to fight for it, to give up the most intimate pieces of themselves, to hold on to it.

However, I didn't say any of that. I just smiled when they both glanced my way.

"Newlyweds?" I asked though I already knew the answer.

"Yes, two days strong," they both replied in perfect sync.

My hurt wanted to mock them, but their unadulterated and slightly obnoxious bliss genuinely made me feel hopeful. Most people pray their entire lives for someone to love them and somehow fate had given me two. Looking back, I wondered how many times happiness was within my reach but eluded me because of my fear, or unwillingness to give up something that I shouldn't hold on to. I promised myself that, from this day forward, I would remember that the only prerequisite to happiness is believing that I am deserving of it.

I had lost every title that I built my entire life around but now the only lens through which I had to view myself were my own. I rested my hand on my stomach and thought about my child, and the role I would have to fulfill as her mother. Closing my eyes one last time, I smiled considering the new beginning that was ahead for both of us. Unlike my child, I had been in this place before, unsure of what was to come next. However, this time, I knew that I would be okay. If the past year taught me anything, it was that fate reveals itself exactly the way that it should. All I had to do was to trust that one day in the future, everything that had occurred would somehow make perfect sense.

I didn't know if I would ever be lucky enough to experience love as I had again, but my child was a reminder that anything was possible. I could only trust that what is meant to be will always find its way to me, even when I least expect it.

EPILOGUE

December 15, 2009

"You've got to be kidding me," Dakota said as she suddenly stopped walking, causing Lola to stumble into a pile of shoveled snow next to them.

"What's wrong with you?" Lola snapped, brushing the wet flakes off her wool pants.

When Dakota didn't respond, she immediately felt guilty. "I'm sorry, Dakota," she said, wiping her eyes. "I can't think straight right now. What's wrong?"

She continued to type a message on her phone. When she finally looked up, she saw what Dakota had seen. He was standing on the other side of the glass doors, talking to the hospital security guard whom she had passed several times over the course of the past few hours. Though she hadn't seen him for over five years, she recognized him instantly.

"You've got to be kidding me," Lola immediately echoed, stopping in her tracks.

"I know," Dakota responded.

They quickened their pace across the parking lot until they were at the hospital's emergency room doors. Peering at him through the paned glass they both wondered the same thing.

"Do you think she has seen him?" Lola asked, worried for her younger sister who had been at the hospital since that morning.

"I hope not," Dakota said, equally afraid of what seeing Gabe might do to Lotus. "What is he doing here? Does he work here?"

Lola looked at Dakota. Her expression spoke for itself.

"How would I know, Dakota? I haven't even mentioned his name to her since the night after she returned from London. Can you please call her and make sure that she is okay?"

Dakota grabbed her cell phone out of her coat pocket and dialed several numbers. When there was no answer, she sent her cousin a text. Lola looked at her impatiently as they waited for a response. When there was none, they both walked into the building.

He was still speaking with the older woman when he saw them walk in. Without warning, Lola grabbed and pulled him away from the security guard until they were back in the frigid, cold air.

"Lola," he said, obviously surprised to see her. "I'm so sorry to hear about Layla. I was about to --"

"Don't do anything," she said, interrupting him.

Dakota was now back outside with them and gave her a warning look from behind Gabe. She reluctantly stood at a distance, leery of what Lola might say.

She shook her head cautiously, "Lola."

Lola ignored her. "Gabe, I don't know what you are doing here and I know that it's none of my business. Lotus is my business, and I will do anything to make sure that she is okay right now. I'm asking you to stay as far away from her as humanly possible. She doesn't need you to be a shoulder that she can cry on just so you can remind her that you are a selfish piece of shit."

"Lola, stop," Dakota said. It wasn't until she walked to Lola's side that she could see Gabe's face. She had only met him once, but she could understand why it took Lotus so long to get over him. Despite what Lola had just said to him, his expression remained empathetic. She looked at him apologetically, but his eyes remained fixed on Lola.

"If your sister needs anything from me, I won't think twice about giving it to her," he responded.

"Then you are just as self-centered as I always thought you were. She needs many things right now, but it's hard for me to believe that you are one of them. If you ever loved her, stay away from her instead of reopening another wound that you don't intend to help heal," Lola told him before Dakota pulled her back into the hospital.

***

"I should have told her," Lola said, as she continued to drive around aimlessly a few miles away from the airport.

"We both should have told her," Dakota agreed.

"I just thought that it would have done more harm than good," Lola tried to convince herself again as she turned into a restaurant's parking lot.

"But she should have known everything before she left," Dakota insisted.

Lola looked at her watch. "It has been over an hour and a half. She had to have gotten on the plane. She would have called us by now if she didn't, right?" she asked, needing assurance. She didn't want to think that she could be the cause of her sister making a mistake that would affect the rest of her life. Her prayer since they had left the Drake Hotel, hours before, was that Lotus was making a decision that she felt in her heart was for the best for her and her child.

"Lola, don't blame yourself. We both made the decision not to tell her all these years. It was over a decade ago, and there has never been a reason to tell her."

"Until now," Lola added.

"Right," Dakota agreed as she stared out of the window.

Lola parked her truck and they waited. She could see the airport from afar but continued to be filled with regret. She believed that she had done the right thing for years to protect her sister, but for the past seven months she wondered, almost every day, if she had made a mistake.

"I wish Gabe had just told her," Lola said, glancing over at Dakota wearily.

Dakota agreed. "I still can't believe that he didn't say anything."

"Layla had just died. Gabe was the last person I expected to see in that hospital," Lola said. "Lotus was in a state of shock. What would you have done?"

"I'm not judging you, Lola. Considering the circumstances, I probably would have told him not to contact her either," she said.

"But considering how much that impacted the way that she felt about him, I just wondered if she deserved to know why he never called her."

"We should have told her," Dakota said, feeling a vibration on her leg.

"I hadn't thought about that conversation until the morning of Lotus' wedding. When I realized that she had been crying, somehow I immediately knew that it was about him."

When Dakota felt her phone vibrate again, she couldn't bring herself to say anything. She had never seen Lola look scared of anything. She could tell by the way that her cousin clenched the steering wheel that she was afraid of how Lotus might feel if she ever found out.

"I'll have to live with the decision I made, and I'm okay with that. But now that Lotus is gone, hopefully, there will never be a reason she would ever have to find out."

Taking her key out of the ignition, she looked over to Dakota again. When her cousin glanced up from her phone, she knew.

"She didn't go with him, did she?" Lola asked, looking down at the phone in Dakota's hand.

Dakota shook her head.

"No, she didn't," Dakota said, unable to push away the sinking feeling in her stomach. "Her text message says to reassure you that she's not going to jump out a window and that she is okay."

Lola sat back in her seat. Before starting her car, she looked back over to Dakota whose grim expression reaffirmed her thoughts.

"We can't tell her." Lola said.

Dakota's somber expression was replaced by one of confusion. "Lola."

"We can't tell her. She's hormonal, alone and emotional. She would never forgive us," Lola repeated as she put her key in the ignition. Even from across the car, Dakota could see her cousin's hands begin to fidget as she held the steering wheel. "What do you think we should do?"

Dakota didn't respond. Instead, she picked up her phone and began to type on its keypad. When she pressed "send" she was nervous, but the burden she felt for far too long slowly began to subside.

"What did you just send?" Lola asked, though she knew her cousin well enough that she had her suspicions.

"I told her that we were on our way," Dakota said, turning to look her nervously. "Then I told her that we had an interesting story to tell her."

Discussion Guide

1) Does "timing" truly determine the fate of relationships?
2) Have you ever suspected that a close friend was in love with someone other than the person she/he was in a relationship with? If so, did you ever express your concerns?
3) Given Lotus' unresolved feelings for Gabe, should she have married Nick?
4) How much should a husband know about his wife's past relationships?
5) The loss of Lotus' sister affected every character. Has grief influenced you to make a life-changing decision that you later regretted?
6) Lotus' sister and cousin played a major role in her decision-making. Was she too dependent on them?
7) Did you anticipate Elizabeth's betrayal?
8) Did Lotus cross the line by agreeing to have lunch with Gabe?

9) Lola and Dakota cautioned Lotus against admitting her indiscretion. Do you agree with their advice?
10) Did Lotus overreact to Nick's acceptance of the Sorbonne-Paris offer?
11) Did Lotus make the right decision about Gabe?
12) Should Lotus have given Nick the envelope?
13) Is it ever okay to keep secrets in relationships?
14) Dakota and Lola's secret justified? Did they make the right decision in the end?
15) Is there any hope for Lotus and Nick in the future? Lotus and Gabe?

Visit
www.kaywsmith.com
for updates on upcoming books, interviews,
and blog posts from the author.